Hannah Jackson

for Nora,
who cares about
books and writers and
stories —a great reader!
best wishes,
Sherry

Hannah Jackson

a novel

SHERRY KAFKA WAGNER

FORT WORTH, TEXAS

On the cover: Late-day scene in rural Gillespie County, Texas.
Carol M. Highsmith, photographer. Courtesy Library of Congress, 30255u.

Library of Congress Control Number: 202094005

TCU Box 298300
Fort Worth, Texas 76129
817.257.7822
www.prs.tcu.edu
To order books: 1.800.826.8911

Design by Julie Rushing

The Texas Traditions Series Number 46
James Ward Lee, Series Editor

For Kim and Adam and Robyn
and
with gratitude for my dear friend,
Lonn Taylor,
who helped give this book a second life

Give her of the fruit of her hands; and let her own works praise her in the gates.

Proverbs 31:31

Preface to the New Edition

When I began writing this book, I was young. Twenty-two years old. It was three years before I finished it. It took two more years for me to get the courage to submit the manuscript to a publisher, and another two years before I held the first copy in my hands. I remember slowly tracing the title with my finger, amazed that words I had written were printed and out in the world.

That was the fall of 1966.

Now, fifty-four years later, there is this new edition of the novel. Much has happened since 1962, the year when the novel ends. In the book, people are beginning to leave rural life and small towns for the cities that now dominate our nation and the world. Some of the fissures that appear in this story are yawning gaps in today's society. Tensions that once moved beneath the surface of communities now surge full-voiced into public spaces. People who were invisible, their voices not heard, their stories not shared, today rightfully demand to be seen and heard, their stories equal with others.

Yet, with much change we still experience the riddle that one person presents to another. Certainly a person is often an enigma to those around them. Can we ever truly know another person? Isn't it sometimes difficult to discern another's motivations—or even our own? Isn't there a mystery in all persons, something deeper than we can readily grasp? And isn't this particularly true for women, who are constrained from presenting a complete self to the world—and to themselves? For me, these abiding questions underlie Hannah Jackson's story.

My dear friend Lonn Taylor believed that this novel deserved a new life. It was he who recommended it to TCU Press. It grieves me that he did not live to see this new edition. He was—and is—a radiance in my life.

I am grateful to TCU Press and its dedicated staff for creating this new edition.

Most of all, I am grateful to you, Dear Reader, for taking this book into your hands. Please read on.

Sherry Kafka Wagner

The Texas Traditions Series
TCU Press

An acclaimed list, the TCU Press Texas Traditions Series is dedicated to promoting Texas literary culture by reprinting classic works of Texas literature that otherwise would disappear from bookstores and libraries. Among the most notable Texas authors the series has brought back into print are Elmer Kelton, Dan Jenkins, Beverly Lowry, Shelby Hearon, Bryan Woolley, Benjamin Capps, Robert Flynn, and Tom Pendleton. In addition to publishing the works of renowned Texas authors, the series also reprints works of authors who are less known, such as Loula Grace Erdman, but whose books evince the highest qualities of literary culture and achievement. The series began under the editorship of William T. Pilkington and continues under James Ward Lee, who himself is a classic Texas tradition.

Hannah Jackson

I

SYE JOHN MORRISON

Let me tell you about Fremond, Texas. You won't find another who knows it better than Sye John. I can see a goodly portion of the main street from this bench in front of Cabot's store where I sit every day. I could lead you through every street in town blindfolded, describe each house, and quote you the names of the people who live in them. Their names ain't all I could tell you.

You see, I've been a peg leg since I was a young man. Over fifty years now. That's a considerable time to sit on a bench and watch one town. The way I figure it, a man's bound to learn something or other in that length of time regardless of who or what he is.

This ain't much of a town, as towns go. Ain't even a county seat. Five, maybe six thousand live here. About seven hundred of these are Mexicans who were here before any of the rest of us came—the true Texans, actually, but Mexicans nonetheless. Still speaking Spanish and clinging to their own ways and their own faith, they live together in the southwest corner of Fremond in rows of small, weathered gray houses with bright flowers growing in the yard. Sometimes I walk through that part of town in the cool of the evening to listen to the music that comes from the open doors of the houses, and to hear the voices calling to each other in that language of theirs which sounds more like music than like words. They fall silent when I go by, watching me with those big dark eyes, crossing themselves as protection against the curse of this big ancient gringo clomping by on his wooden stump. They're a proud, secret people leading a hidden life in this one small corner of my town.

As for the others, we've got all kinds of people here. Just like any other place. Big people, little people, tall, thin, short, fat, good, bad—all kinds of people. Take your pick. Some ain't worth killing but then occasionally, very rarely, we have a saint among us. Lyndale Ethridge was one. He was the schoolmaster here about fifty years ago, and a saint as sure as you're born.

If you don't believe me, just ask Cyrus Barton over to the drug store. Cyrus is one of the few people around here who can remember Lyndale Ethridge. Like most towns, we don't have a long memory for those saintly ones among us. But I'll lay good odds that there ain't a kid over six years of age in this entire town what can't point out to you the tree where a mob of citizens lynched three cattle rustlers over a hundred years ago. We are an ordinary people and, like all people, we find vice more interesting than virtue.

This street here is Main Street. It don't really have no name, but it's the main street in town. From where I'm sitting in front of Cabot's I can see from one end of the street to the other. Down at the far end is the railroad station. Looks like any other railroad station in these parts, a yellow building with brown trim. It has a waiting room with a potbellied stove that hasn't been used for the last twenty years. Not since they brought natural gas in here by pipeline. There's a little room where the stationmaster works, and a good-sized baggage and shipping room. You can see how the street rises up over the railroad tracks. Once over the tracks it meanders off to meet the new highway. The railroad station marks the end of Fremond proper and the beginning of the world outside.

At the other end of the street is the First Church. The church is set right square in the middle of things and the street has to divide to go around it. People passing through here sometimes mistake it for a courthouse. It's got that kind of blocky, official look. It's made of a granite stone that comes from Marble Falls, another town not too far from here. It's a pretty enough stone off to itself, but it makes up drab. Drab, but solid, that's our First Church. Got plain windows in it; no colored glass for us. That would be too heathen for the folks around here. They leave colored windows and other such trimmings to the little Catholic chapel over in the southwest corner. The only thing fancy about the First Church is the steeple, if you can call it that. Actually, it's more of a squatty little cupola stuck on the front of the building just above the doors.

The doors. Now we've finally hit on something special. They are the finest doors I've ever seen. Two inches thick and made of solid oak fitted with brass. Closed against you, they remind you how puny you are, how small your strength. And you somehow expect them to open upon some vision as glistening and mysterious as Jehovah Himself, seated upon His throne, white beard flowing, while cherubim sing and an angel flies down to touch your lips with a burning coal. Yet when the doors are opened, they reveal nothing more than the foyer of the church with racks for coats and hats and umbrellas and overshoes and a table for neat stacks of paper with the order of service printed upon them. Inside, the church is plain and simple. Two sections of pews with a center aisle and an aisle along each outside wall. A red carpet down the center aisle. The pulpit carpeted in the same red. There's a choir loft and two large wooden chairs cushioned in red behind the pulpit. Down front is a communion table made of the same heavy dark wood as the chairs.

Of course, the church don't have to be ugly just because it ain't fancy. Some of the prettiest buildings I've ever seen ain't fancy. But this church of ours ain't pretty. It's too square and heavy and dark. Still, the sunlight has a way of coming through the high windows in long slants of pale, pale yellow that makes a man conscious of the breath in his throat. But I suppose that's a beauty that don't have nothing to do with buildings.

Between the church and the railroad station lie all the rest of the town's businesses. Two rows of brick and wooden buildings, some single-storied, some double, facing each other across a street that started out as a wagon trail of hard-packed dirt, then became gravel, then brick, and now pavement. Old, dirty, weather-worn buildings, many of them with rotting wooden porches that extend out over the sidewalks and rest upon slender poles. Across the street lies Cyrus Barton's drug store, which he took over after his father killed himself with an overdose of the drug to which he was addicted. Like I said, Fremond has its share of the vices. Next to Barton's is Rostov's Candy Shop which is owned by old lady Rostov, as deaf and as mean an old lady as ever drawed breath. Makes fine candy, though. And we got a hardware store, a dress shop which is run by the Misses Willa Mae and Sarah Sue Raymond, a variety store, a combination bus station and café, and a saddlery on that side of the street.

This side has an office building where the two doctors, the dentist, and our three lawyers have their offices, a feed store, two groceries, a newspaper office, the First State Bank—housed in the grandest building in town, especially since the big remodeling they did six years ago—the post office, a bakery, and Cabot's General Store. Off the side street that runs beside the railroad station is a lumberyard, a flower shop, and a furniture store. That's the sum total of Fremond's commercial enterprises, excepting three gas stations and a motel out on the new highway. Those are the only new businesses been built in Fremond in many a year.

From my bench here I can see the entire street from church to railroad station. I can even see the cars that turn off to go to the lumberyard, the flower shop, and the furniture store. Nothing much goes on from morning to evening without Sye John spying it out. Last year on my birthday I came down about eight-thirty in the morning like I've been doing for years, and I found this bright red bench here where the old one had been. Brand-new it was and shining like the morning dew. Even has a plaque on it here that says, *This Bench Is the Property of Sye John Morrison Who Has Earned it.* Moffett Tremayne had gotten together with some of my friends around here and planned this birthday surprise for me. Tickled pink with themselves, they were. Outside of my peg and a little box of remembrances in my room at the boarding house, this is all in the world that I own. But it's enough, my friend. It's enough.

MOFFETT TREMAYNE

I attended Hannah Jackson's funeral this morning. After the funeral I stopped to mail Emmaline's letter to our son, Gregory. Then I crossed the street and climbed the stairs to my office where I have spent the last five hours sitting in my swivel chair staring out the window.

This is not an easy thing for me to do. Unfortunately I am cursed with one of those Puritan consciences which beats a continual tattoo of guilt through my mind when I waste twenty minutes of my precious, God-given allotment of time on this earth in "useless activity." After all, is not Sloth one of the Seven Sins? And what activity could be more useless than spending five hours gazing out the window at the main street of Fremond, Texas?

Once I asked Sye John what he did every day on that infernal bench of his. "Watch," he said. "Watch what?" I asked. "Watch this town of mine," he answered.

Well, I hope to hell he sees more than I do.

So we buried Hannah Jackson today. An end to that life and to that story. Or is it? Beginnings and endings have always been a source of confusion for me. How in God's name do you tell one from the other, or are they both the same?

Either way, Hannah Jackson is buried, I am middle-aged, my son has become a man and gone away, my window reveals nothing to me that I have not seen before, and I know that despair does not always hide in the dark corners of night like a beast ready to pounce, but often it can be spied from my window prowling the streets in the hard, sparkling, metallic light of a fall day. Still my window reveals nothing to me of death, and I know little more of life.

I wonder what Hannah would tell me of life and death, now that she is done with living and dying? What would she say of this life of ours? Is it "useful activity"?

I remember somebody once said to me that grief is like a fine coating of dust and ashes laid uniformly over our once gleaming, glittering world. And yet it is not death or grief or despair that holds me immobile at this window but life itself, the strangeness of it. It is not death that is the mystery but living.

Tell me, Hannah Jackson, not of your death, but of the mystery that was your life.

TERRELL L. JACKSON

What a strange and twisted plant human love is! How glorious the flowering, how bitter the fruit, how deep the roots! And how eternally painful its withering and its death.

I loved once in my life, and now my love is dead. Today I buried my Hannah, my wife, buried that one whose soul was in some mysterious and frightening way tangled together with my own. And I have not wept. I cannot weep; I will not weep. Some grief there is that lies beyond the remedy of tears, and it is this grief that falls from the dead growth of love and litters the world. Grief, my Hannah, is a dead dry leaf scratching along the ground, tossed by every wind, shattered into dust by every chance encounter with memory.

My love for you brought me grief, Hannah, as inevitably as the autumn follows the summer. The birth of love is but the prophecy of its death, and what one would hold is what one must lose. I buried your wasted, disease-ridden body that had held for me the mystery and glory of each new day, and I did not shed a single tear for all the torment and pain and joy and horror and bliss of loving you.

Why you should have been the very center of my heart and life is something that I suppose I shall never understand. I fought you. I would have destroyed you if I could. I knew the extent of your cruelty, the terror of your weapons, and the mercilessness of your tormenting. Yet my love endured and continued long after I had closed myself against you, and even as your coffin was lowered into the ground I could feel that same love welling up within me. Why should that be? Was it because I also knew your tenderness, the way you marveled at pleasure, accepting it as a child accepts a gift, the way you trembled at the tiniest glimpse of happiness and clutched against you the merest shred of hope?

I do not know why it should have been thus, but I can say to all the world that I loved Hannah beyond my capacity for knowledge or understanding or comprehension. And there is nothing that she did or could have done that would have changed that.

Listen, my Hannah. I have something more to say. I bless your name. I bless you.

REVEREND STEPHEN LONGSTREET

Life in Fremond, Texas, in 1921 was simpler than life is today. More innocent, somehow. Or perhaps the innocence I remember and attribute to that
time was simply my own. I was a very young man, newly married, in my
first pastorate.

Looking about me today, I marvel at the young ministers. They go into
their first church only after years of study and training, not only in theol-
ogy, but in psychology and sociology and any number of other disciplines
that were almost unknown to a young man in a small Texas community in
the Year of Our Lord 1921. They are aware that it takes more to serve God
than a desire. I was not.

I sometimes wonder if they, with their superior knowledge and training,
with their more sophisticated language and tools, will be able to minister
to a Hannah Jackson. Or must they be compelled, as I have been, to carry
the memory of one such as Hannah throughout their lives in order to serve
at all?

I was a country boy, born on a farm to hardworking, God-fearing parents. When I told them that I felt called to be a minister of the Gospel, my
mother wept, my father shook my hand, and I packed my clothes in a cardboard box and went off to the nearest denominational college. I was then
twenty-two years old. Four and a half years later—four and a half years of
shoveling coal and cutting wood and selling Bibles and sweeping floors and
skipping meals and scrounging books and sleeping in the basement of a
kindly teacher's home—I emerged from college with a young wife and my
first pastoral assignment—Fremond, Texas.

"Lead on, Lord," I said. "Thy servant is prepared."

And what had I learned in those four years that so well prepared me to
take on the awesome mantle of Messenger of the Most High God? Words,
that's all. Lots of words. Words like Destruction and Hell and Grace and
Salvation and Sin, Sin, Sin. I knew how to form words into a sermon, a

wedding ceremony, a funeral, how to administer the sacraments, how to phrase a prayer. I knew all the words.

"Lead on, Lord. Thy servant has learned his lines. He is ready to play his part."

I wasn't, of course. But I had no way of knowing that until I became entangled in the life of Hannah. It was she who brought me to the realization that a man is never prepared to serve his God, that there is no preparation, that the most one can do is carry in his heart the prayer, "Speak, Lord, for Thy servant heareth." Carry that prayer inside him, an unceasing litany, while he waits, submissive, with faith that God may find a way to use him.

Life *was* simpler in Fremond then. I'm sure of it. At least the rules were more clearly defined. Take the issue of divorce. The position of the church then was no different from what it is now, but how very different the practice! In the small rural communities of the South, divorce was still a scandalous, almost ruinous tragedy. Most of the churches in these towns had formed a stringent moral code out of their strict fundamentalist view of the Bible and of the doctrines of the church. The rules of conduct were harshly enforced by a clergy spouting hellfire and damnation and condemning all the earth and they that dwelled therein.

These churches had a simple view of divorce. It was wrong, totally and absolutely. A man and woman married, and they were married till death did them part. Amen. Regardless of pain, suffering, loss of love, etc., etc., they were married. And even if the law said they could be divorced, they were still united in the eyes of God and should conduct themselves as married people.

Now, I am not saying that marriages were happier then, but such a strict interpretation of the church's position on marriage caused the people to do much less about unhappiness. Divorce was not unknown, but it was rare. Many married couples lived in a perpetual literal state of divorcement, but they did not actually go to court and obtain a legal decree. They might live together in complete isolation and silence, but live together they did. There were very few brave and hardy souls who risked the scandal of divorce. The general feeling in such communities as Fremond was that, if such a scandal as divorce did occur, the parties to it might possibly be accepted back into the life of the community if they never remarried. There were two acceptable modes of conduct: marriage or celibacy. Anything else was Sin, pure and simple.

Take Miss Addie Langford, for instance. One of my most faithful parishioners while I was in Fremond, she was a wistful, gentle woman who sat in the sixth pew on the right every service. The congregation thought well of Miss Addie, admired her tender kindness, her faithfulness to the church. I suppose some even loved her for her thoughtfulness and warmth, but none would have suggested that she participate in any active manner in the life of the church. For Miss Addie was divorced.

During the thirty-seven years that Miss Addie taught music in Fremond, every organist at our church was one or another of her students. But at no time was Miss Addie herself asked to play for a service, nor would she have accepted if the invitation had been offered. She was divorced, and, because of that, she must sit in her pew and wince as her pupils stumbled their way through music that would have flowed easily and beautifully from beneath her fingers. Occasionally she would move a long slender finger in rhythm or nod her head as she urged them on, her thin face drawn with the intensity of her concentration on each note.

When she was a young girl Miss Addie had gone off to New York City to study music. While there she had fallen in love with a fellow student, a young composer, and she married him. Her father, indignant that his only daughter had married without his consent and married a penniless Yankee musician at that, had gone to New York, brought her home, obtained a divorce for her, then installed her as housekeeper in his big Victorian home where she waited on him hand and foot until his death, repaid only by her father's eternal abuse and by the dubious pleasure of introducing the young of Fremond to the joys of music. Her father never forgave her for what he called "Addie's terrible mistake."

Soon after my arrival in Fremond I called at the house and we had tea together, Addie, myself, and Copeland Langford, who was then eighty years old and confined to a wheelchair. He was a frail, cranky old man, ill, and rapidly sinking into senility. But he roused himself enough to give me a lecture on the ingratitude of children, the dangers that a city holds for young women, and a treatise on the reasons a man should "keep his daughter in the house where he can keep an eye on her." All the time he droned on in his harsh querulous voice, Miss Addie sat beside him, face flushed and gray head bent, her thin hands folded in her lap except for the few times she raised one hand to replace his shawl which, in his vehemence, he had shaken from his shoulders. Several times I noticed that she blinked rapidly in an effort to hold back tears.

It was during that single visit that I first heard her play. After her father had left the room for his afternoon nap, I asked her if she would play for me. And, sitting at the piano, in the dim faded light of that dark heavy room, she did. Something by Schumann, I think. Her tall thin body hunched over the keys, her eyes closed, the fingers moving with a will of their own. I have never heard music shaped more beautifully, more lovingly, never heard it molded with more grace and feeling than on that afternoon when I sat in that draped and darkened parlor holding a cold cup of tea. When she was through, she sat for a moment immobile, then turned to me, spreading her pale hands in the dim light and smiling slightly.

"That's how it is, Mr. Longstreet," she said. "That's how it is."

I thanked her for the tea and the music and left. The next day I wrote a note, offering her the use of the organ at the church whenever she cared to play it. Many, many times after that I sat in my study and listened to Miss Addie playing Bach, the music swelling and racing and pouring, echoing through the empty church, making it throb like something living. But, gifted as she was, respected and liked as she was, Miss Addie could only play in an empty church, for she was divorced.

Such was life in Fremond, Texas, in 1921, when Hannah fell in love with a married man and he divorced his wife in order to marry her.

II

GREGORY TREMAYNE

I had gone to Chicago to visit a girl I had met last summer at a resort. The girl had been as pretty as I remembered and the weekend all I had hoped. So I found myself standing opposite the ticket desks at the airport feeling satisfied and a little proud. I was twenty-one, six feet tall in my socks, and wearing a new sports jacket. What more could an American male ask?

Something about airports, railroad terminals, bus depots, any place of departure has always fascinated and intrigued me. When I was a kid at home in Texas, I used to walk down to the bus depot and buy an ice cream bar at the counter. Then I would sit on the dusty bench outside the back door and wait for the clumsy buses to come lumbering up the narrow back alley. Nobody interesting ever seemed to get on or off those buses. Just some old farmer from East Texas coming to visit his married daughter and carrying his clothes in a cardboard suitcase and the remains of his lunch wrapped in a newspaper. There might be some Mexicans or a colored person getting off, and one time there was even a little blonde girl in a fluffy pink and white dress—Mrs. Everson's granddaughter from Dallas. But on the whole, nobody exciting rode the buses to or from our town. The exciting faces, the faces that kept me on the bench after the ice cream was gone, were the faces looking down at me from the fly-specked windows of the bus, looking down emptily, curiously, at the back door of the depot, watching the driver swagger inside to speak to Mattie Blair who ran the bus station and to drink from the electric fountain, the only cold water fountain in town. Even when I was a kid there was something about those faces, ghostly heads with no bodies, that stirred me, made me feel the motion of the earth.

Now I was twenty-one and satisfied with myself, even proud, yet still excited by the faces of the travelers, seeing in their rushing, moving, hurrying, the turning of the globe, the rising of Rome, Tokyo, Berlin, Moscow, toward the sun, each in its term and each within man's reach. I was a traveler too, a face at the window, disinterested and curious, looking out at a town I could never know or belong to, free for a moment from the demands of earth and time. Four hundred miles from the midwestern campus where I now lived, fourteen hundred miles from the Texas town with its ice cream bars and bench outside the bus depot. I was twenty-one and a traveler living only on the credit of my face as it moved through space, free.

I was watching the ticket agents writing the arrival times on the boards behind their booths when she walked into view. She had her back to me. Her hair was gathered neatly and discreetly into a knot on the back of her head, and she was dressed smartly in black. Yet I recognized her at once. And because I was twenty-one and satisfied with myself, I hesitated only a moment before I approached her.

"Miss Secoria Jackson," I said close to her ear, "you are a long way from home." She swung quickly toward the sound of my voice and puckered her forehead with the effort of remembering. Her face was thinner than I had remembered and there were lines marking other efforts the face had made, efforts at remembering and efforts at forgetting.

"Greg Tremayne." Her voice had not changed at all. It still had the raw, hoarse edges that had caused Sye John Morrison to say of her when she was still only a girl in her teens, "She'll never be a lady, that one. That voice, it could never say lady things. That's a voice for swearing and loving, Greg boy, two things ladies don't do."

She put her hand on my arm and pulled me around into the light. "Gregory Tremayne, you've grown up."

I smiled and answered, "It was inevitable, Miss Secoria, inevitable."

Yes, it was inevitable that I would grow up, Secoria Jackson, just as it was inevitable that you, my first love, would grow older, and that I would meet you in the airport in Chicago and that we would chat about the embassy in London where you worked and about the university where I studied and about the weather and any other thing around which we could both fit our words. Yet never talking about the things we both knew and which in some way tied us to the duty of standing still together for a moment in a place dedicated to motion. We were two travelers, faces free on the air, moving as the earth moved, overtaking any place, any time, able to reach to Moscow or Rome, yet suddenly finding that there were anchors, there were bodies, left behind perhaps, but still part of us. And as we talked about the jet time from New York to London, the dust of a Texas town swirled about us. As I marveled at the neat manicured fingers nervously tapping a cigarette, I saw the sunburned hands that once had broken my first horse for me.

"I hope to come to Europe this summer," my words said. But my mind was saying, Secoria Jackson, you're still a handsome woman, but I am no longer in love with you. Where has she gone, that untamed girl I loved, riding on her half-wild horse with her blazing eyes and her hair tousled and windblown? There are only ashes in your eyes now; your mouth is thin and tight. And the fury that used to be in your body and your hands and which cried out of everything you did, where is it? Is it in ashes too? You're still a handsome woman, Secoria Jackson, but I no longer love you.

The tin voice of the dispatcher announced the flight for New York. I walked with Miss Secoria Jackson to the gate, promising to phone her when I was in London and dragging with me all the memories of her that were infested with Texas sun and Texas dirt. Still we did not speak of it until she reached the gate. Then she looked up at me quickly and said, "I've just been to Fremond, Greg. The bishop's mother died."

Then Fremond rose around us and we were not free, we were not faces floating past, we were not free and never would we be. Never would we be.

SECORIA JACKSON

Why did I have to see Gregory Tremayne in the airport? Why, why, why? Because nothing is ever finished, because nobody is ever buried, because everywhere I go I trail behind me all the things I remember—or is it all the things I have forgotten? But there was Greg looking at me with little boy eyes in a man's face, and I was saying to him, "The bishop's mother died," wasting on his youth all the clever bitterness of that remark.

The bishop's mother died, I said, but Gregory Tremayne is too young to have ears tuned to irony so he only heard sorrow and pressed my arm. He pressed *my* arm, like I was the one in mourning. Did you know that, Hannah? That boy, that child grown up, he thought I was in mourning for you! As if anybody could ever mourn you. You, lying there so magnificently triumphant, so scornful and strong, dying there as though death were your final victory. Nobody would dare mourn your leaving, Hannah. None of us were brave enough. No, we were left like cowards to mourn ourselves, to mourn our defeats, to crawl off and lick our wounds and contemplate our scars knowing that there would never be another battle, that you had won them all.

So I left Fremond forever. A final leaving with my nostrils full of the smell of funeral flowers and my head warmed by brandy that Father smuggled to me, and I did not look back. At last, I said, it is final. The silver cord cut, the invisible links broken. It is over, over, over. I rode off on the bus, looking neither to the right nor the left, but with my eyes staring straight ahead, blazing the trail of my departure, while on every side of me the past flashed by, faster and faster. The bishop's mother was dead.

I left Fremond forever, yet it rose again in the Chicago airport. And it will rise again in London or Paris or New York or some place whose name I do not yet know. It will rise in other little boy faces that have grown up while I was not looking, and in faces I have never yet seen and which answer to names I may never know. So you see, Hannah, you go on winning, even from the grave. And I am still defeated every day. Defeated by faded photographs that make up the contents of that hidden purse each of us carries with us, our own private oblivion, suddenly spilling open in unlikely places, catching us off guard in airports and hotels, in morning sun or at night. Every time it spills its neglected, half-forgotten contents into our consciousness, we are defeated by the pain of what was. Yet, Hannah, the final victory, the final irony: we shall be even more defeated when there is no longer pain in memory. When we no longer fear nor regret, but simply walk among the ashes with only the warmth of brandy in our heads to know that we are alive.

Yes, Gregory Tremayne, the bishop's mother died. And one night when we were drinking together, I suggested to Father that we engrave on the tombstone, Love Conquers All. How does that strike your young ears?

SYE JOHN MORRISON

Well, as the darkies say, they had the funeralizing today. Buried Hannah Jackson right on top the rise in the graveyard. Right next to Timothy they buried her, leaving space on the other side for Terrell when he decides to join her.

They're putting up a stone for her too, John Cabot says. Just a simple one, her name and the dates. A hundred years from now some kids hunting crows will see that stone and read her name and not know one thing about her. That's what I said to John Cabot and he answered me while he was dusting stock, "Hannah left her memorial in other ways, Sye John. She was one of those women who leaves her mark on a town."

Well, I have to give her that. She left her mark, she sure as hell did. And the likes of John Cabot, always dusting the stock and tying on his apron and worrying about money will never see it and never understand it and couldn't do anything about it if he did, any more than I could.

"You going to the funeral?" John asked me. "No," I said, "I've done seen enough things in my lifetime. Enough of flowers and preachers and funerals." But ole John, he closed things down at the store and brushed off his black coat and went out to pay his last respects.

REVEREND STEPHEN LONGSTREET

The older I get, the harder it is to understand the ways of man. And it seems downright foolish for a person to even *try* to learn the ways of God. I've been a minister for forty-three years, but I've never gotten used to funerals.

I would not have gone today if Terrell Jackson had not telephoned me and asked that I come and lead in prayer. I must admit that I was surprised. I thought the last thing Terrell would have wanted was another preacher, what with every preacher within fifty miles coming anyway because it was the funeral of the mother of a bishop. Terrell said, "You knew her when she was young." And I answered, "I'll come."

Yes, I knew her when she was young and hungering after truth. But I wasn't so old myself. No, I was young enough to think the truth was easy and simple. Perhaps that is what I should have prayed for today—forgiveness. Forgiveness for thinking that life is simple, that love is easy, that faith hovers around us ready for the asking.

I'm very tired now. Maude said that I was a silly old thing for saying I would take part in the funeral. "You know," she said, "how tired you get. They can just get some other minister to pray."

And I said, "No, they can't, Maude, because all those others are too young to realize that praying is an art, and like all art it takes experience, knowledge, proficiency, and then that extra something that is variously called talent, brilliance, genius, and which I like to call a flash of glory." But Maude only answered that I would never have any sense whatsoever. Well, that's true enough. Few of us ever have any real sense of anything or concerning anything. Even fewer have the courage to live as though they understand the ways of man. And only a tiny elect dare live as though they understand the ways of God.

That was how Hannah Jackson lived.

LETTER FROM EMMALINE TREMAYNE
TO HER SON, GREGORY,
WRITTEN NOVEMBER 3, 1960

Dear Greg,

I am sending the shirts you asked for, but I do not think they will be heavy enough for the cold weather. You would probably do better to buy some inexpensive shirts there, wool or something at Penney's or some place cheap. They would do to keep you warm when you were outdoors for sports and things and also do for class. Then you could save your good shirts for dress-up.

I am sorry that I can't write much today but we have all been saddened by the death of Hannah Jackson. She was such a fine person, an inspiration to everybody and so brave while she was ill. Her family was here. I saw Secoria and said a few words to her. She is changed, very much the city girl if you know what I mean. She remembered you and the horses you used to ride at her house. Terrell stayed sober through the funeral, which was a miracle in itself. You know how Daddy worries about Terrell because he was once a good friend of your grandfather and your father and a very fine person. Just goes to show you what drink can do to a person. Do you remember the oldest boy Mark? He was here, a very handsome man. He is a bishop now, you know. He seemed to take his mother's death very hard. The whole thing was so sad to me, but I was glad that she at least had this one son that she could be proud of. So many things in this world don't turn out like we hope they will.

Daddy sends his love. We are glad that you are working hard. We miss you and want you to come home for Christmas if you can. Let me know when you get the shirts.

> Much love to my big boy,
> Mother

ENTRY IN THE DIARY OF
MARK THOMAS JACKSON,
NOVEMBER 3, 1960

This was the day of Mother's funeral. We buried her next to Timothy. Last night when Secoria had too much to drink she screamed that she would not let us bury Mother beside Timothy, that we could not do that to Tim. But today she was quiet and did not mention it again.

I noticed that the funeral service which is so familiar to me as a minister sounded completely new and strange, as though I were hearing it for the first time. There was a weight and density to the words that I had never suspected before. Perhaps there is a dimension and meaning to them that only the sorrowing can know.

Man of Sorrows. Today I caught a glimpse of the terror and majesty of such a name. Could it be that those of us who are immersed in the service of Christ have forgotten that He was the Man of Sorrows? We know the ritual of sorrow so well that we do not often consider the terrible truth behind the ceremony. Sorrow. It is woven into the very texture of each life and colors all things, even our love. *Especially* our love.

Dad drove Secoria to the bus depot. He was very sorry to see her go, because he feels that he will never see her again. I'm going to stay here at the ranch with Dad for a few days. Partly because I think that he needs somebody and partly because there are many old questions about myself and my family which this period of trial and grief seem to have uncovered again. During one of the many painful scenes that occurred between us (one of them while Mother was struggling to grasp her last few breaths), Secoria said to me that I had never dared take a good look at myself, at Mother, at any of the family. "You've always had scales on your eyes, Mark," she said. Maybe she is right. Or maybe it is all part of seeing through a glass darkly—

TERRELL L. JACKSON

Tomorrow is my birthday. I will be sixty-eight years old. To celebrate my birthday I will go to the bank and sign over papers to Morris Hufstadt. Surely that must tell something about how I've spent sixty-eight years on this earth, the fact that I'm selling a section of land that my great-grandfather had homesteaded. The first Terrell Jackson, too hot-blooded for the gentle Virginia manners, came into Texas hell-bent on founding a dynasty and instead produced one gentle circuit judge who in his turn begat one flashy gambler who begat the second Terrell Jackson, rancher, and that second Terrell Jackson, the only one to follow in the old settler's footsteps, he it is who is losing the ranch that cost the old man his life. Yes, I'm the only rancher the old man ever had; yet I'm the one who has betrayed him and done what even the judge and the gambler didn't do. I'm selling his land.

That's the fact of it. The land is being sold and the reasons make no difference whatsoever. Tomorrow the papers will be signed and in a month or so (Morris will wait awhile; ranchers are discreet about land) the signs on the cattle guards will come down and in a year or two people will have reorganized their thinking and will no longer speak of Turkey Bend Ranch going all the way to the creek.

What do you think of that, Hannah? Turkey Bend Ranch no longer goes to Lager Creek. I once said to you that there was comfort in knowing that I could ride a horse for an entire day and not cover all my land and you said that land would slip away and I said not while I watch it and you said simply that land would slip away and you were right. But there is more to it than that, Hannah. Earth slips away, but so does heaven and so does love and youth and life itself and then what does a man do? He betrays his heritage and himself and all he stands for and when he is old he doubts everything that he has ever done and stood for, and if he is lucky or wise he becomes a stoic and if he is unlucky or stubborn or foolish he may drink too much.

There is one more thing to be said between us, Hannah. One thing I didn't tell you. That is the fact that you didn't win because you were right, but you won because I let you, because I loved you more than I loved right. Because I loved you more than I ever loved anything or anybody, including the land, and it was this love for you that made me lose everything worth the having—my ranch, my children, and finally you yourself. Even, perhaps, my own soul. I will, no doubt, die an old man, ugly, dirty, and people shall say dead of drink or dead of age or heart disease or whatever and nobody will suspect that I really died of love.

But you, Hannah, you died because there was nothing else for you to do.

III

SYE JOHN MORRISON

I can still remember the first time I ever saw Hannah Jackson, only it was a long time before she was Hannah *Jackson*. She was a little towheaded kid, holding to her mother's skirt. I ain't quite sure, but I think it was in the fall about fifty years ago. It's sure funny the things a man'll remember, the little things that ain't much good to him. The big things, they're the ones that get blurred when you get old. I guess maybe that's because when you're old it's too much trouble to remember things that cost you in feelings.

I guess I remember about seeing Hannah that time because it has come to mind so often since. Whenever I see a picture of some kid drinking one of them soft drinks I think about that day when Hannah came up and sat down on my bench with me. I was still a young man then, but I had already lost my leg and had the peg. It must have been about noontime because I was working at the lumberyard then and every noon I played checkers out in front of Cabot's store with Len Riggs.

"I'm waiting for my cedar chopper to come by," Len said. "Got a man coming in to do my cedar."

"Where's he coming from?"

"Coming up here from Burnet."

"Gonna camp out at your place?" I asked, thinking I would sure as hell hate to camp on Len Rigg's land or cut his cedar or do much of anything for him. Len was one of those men who always had a gripe, one of those narrow-eyed men with a twisted mouth that whined at you. Funny thing about that. I played checkers with Len for 'long about six years. We played every working day, out in front of Cabot's store, but I never did like him. And I never beat him four days in a row, either.

"Yeah. Gonna put a tent down by the springs. Probably asking for trouble with a chopper living on the place, but that damn cedar's taking over. A man's gotta do something. Guess I oughta get a job in a lumberyard like you got, something steady and easy."

"Your move," I said, thinking to myself, I'm going to beat you today, Len Riggs. Because I was still a young man and it didn't set easy with me when I was put in my place. And that was what he was doing. Saying to me, you are a peg leg, Sye John, a peg leg to sit on a bench and play checkers with, but you don't own any land and you ain't got no real work that's fit for a man.

I would have beat him, too, only they came driving up in front of the store. They were in a wagon, the three of them, sitting up on the seat with the man in the middle driving the one mule.

"I'm looking for Mr. Len Riggs," the man said.

"You found him," Len answered.

They got down from the wagon then, and Len walked out to the edge of the sidewalk where the man was tying the mule to the post. I suppose that I would have put the checkers in the box, folded the board, gone inside to put them under the counter, and talked with James Cabot until time to get back to the yard. That would have been the usual thing. But like I said, I was a young man then and I had seen the woman.

A man with a peg leg does an awful lot of watching, and he sees an awful lot of people. But I ain't never, before or since, seen a woman like Mora Troxler. She woulda made a watcher out of any man. She got down off that wagon, then walked around the back and helped the little girl down while I just sat there, watching, with the checkers in my hand.

It wasn't that she was so pretty or anything. I suppose when you come right down to it, Hannah grew up to be a pretty gal, prettier than her mother ever was. But there was something about the way the woman walked, something about the way she lifted her arms to take that girl down that stopped a man with his hand in midair and made him look so hard he durn near forgot where he was. She was a tall woman, high-colored—I think she must have been part Indian—and she walked like nothing except maybe a deer, quiet and deliberate, but more like she wasn't moving but just being blown along. She fixed the girl's hair, and they whispered together beside the wagon for a while with Len and the man talking business up by the mule and with me sitting on the bench, watching. Finally, the little girl came up to sit on the bench and Mora walked by me and into the store.

It's been fifty years, but I can still remember all that. I can remember, too, the face and the eyes of Mora Troxler as she passed the bench, probably as well or better than any of the other faces I've seen going into Cabot's store. Her face had big strong bones, and the skin looked stretched over them. It wasn't the soft kind of face that a woman usually has, but one that looked as though it had all been made of matching pieces so that everything fit together in the easiest possible way, and there was not one extra wrinkle or fold. But if the face was clear in outline, it was because it had to be in order to balance the extravagance of her eyes. One time, old Pat, the railroad brakeman, told me that God must've had smudgy fingers when he put in the eyes of Irish girl babies. Well, that's the kind of eyes Mora Troxler had, smudgy and shadowed, secret and startling. Yessir, I can remember that face awfully well, and I only saw it about three times.

When the woman had gone into the store, I suddenly felt the weight of the checkers in my hand and turned back to the box lying beside me. The little girl was sitting there, still and quiet, looking down at the ground. She was thin and small with long blonde braids.

"Hello, Susie," I said, just as I always did to the little kids that came round the store and they always laughed up to me protesting that their name was Ruth or Jane or Betty, but this one simply sat and folded her hands in her lap. "You came a long way in that wagon," I went on, waiting for her to look up so that I could see if those remarkable eyes could possibly have repeated themselves. Still she sat folding and refolding her hands. "Listen, Susie, I bet we could walk inside Cabot's store here and find some nice cold sarsaparilla which would taste pretty good if you're thirsty after coming all that way." She still didn't look at me, but she stood up and reached out with one hand to help the peg-legged man get up. And when I took Hannah's hand that day, I felt like I did once when I was a boy and, after carefully inching through the tall grass down by Lager Creek, I caught and held a trembling little bird.

ENTRY IN THE DIARY OF
MARK THOMAS JACKSON,
NOVEMBER 4, 1962

Dad is bothered with insomnia and likes to breakfast early. I got up this morning so that we could breakfast together on the veranda as we did when I was a child. The hills were purple in the early light and the air had the faint edge of winter to it. I forget from one homecoming to another how lovely this land can be in the early part of the day.

Dad had some business in town so I was left alone in the house. I walked all around in it, feeling like the stranger I am. There is a sadness for me in the fact that in this house where my mother lived since she came here as a bride there seemed to be no object that had stored up some essence of her. The silence of the house was oppressive to me. It seemed to mock me, to cry out to me that I never knew her. Yes, I loved her. Yes, she was a great influence on me and upon my life. But she was a stranger. Perhaps that is why I must stay with Dad for a while. I must make some attempt to see beyond the masks that I have always accepted as my family.

When I could stand the house no longer, I took the pickup and drove down Lager Creek to the double springs where Mother camped with her family when they first came to Fremond. Here, for the first time since her death, I seemed to recapture her in my memory.

ENTRY IN THE DIARY OF
MARK THOMAS JACKSON,
JUNE 21, 1934

Today was my sister's birthday. She was six years old. When school starts she will go to school. Mother took Secoria, Tim, and me down to the two springs place on a picnic. Secoria found a turtle and brought him home. She named him Perkie. That is a silly name for a turtle.

Mother told us a story about when she was a little girl. Her mother gave her to a lady called Aunt Minnie to bring up because our grandmother was sick. This made our mother sad because she didn't know why she had been given away. It must have been fun camping by the springs like Mother did when she was little. She said that she could wake up and smell the smoke from the campfire.

My mother is very pretty with her hair shining. I will always love her and not make her sad like when she was little.

Tomorrow Daddy is going to let me go with him to vaccinate some cattle. I have to learn about things like that so I can take care of this ranch when I grow up.

MINNIE CLEMENS

I was getting on in age when I decided to take Hannah Troxler to raise. Now a woman close to seventy years old had no business on this earth taking a little girl to bring up, I know. And if I hadn't known it, I would have heard so from all my friends. That's how it is with friends. They never know enough about you to advise you how to live your life, but they do know enough to think they *should* advise you.

Well, I may have had no right to that child, but she was offered to me and I took her and loved her just like she was my own and like I had a right to her. And I can tell all my friends that I was never sorry.

I was stringing up the morning glory vines over the back porch when Mora Troxler came into the yard. I guess I looked as surprised as I felt because she stopped and lowered her head and just stood there in the yard waiting for me to say something. I guess we stood that way almost a full minute before I had sense enough to ask her in, but it surprised me so. I had only seen her once before and it never occurred to me that she would come walking into my yard one September morning.

Yes, I had seen her only once before, one morning at church, but that was all you had to see her to remember her. She was a lovely woman with pride like an arrow. She may have been the wife of a drunk cedar chopper, but she was a lovely woman.

Well, I finally got sense enough to ask her in, and when we were sitting on the porch drinking iced tea, I realized that she must have walked into town from the springs, a long way in the heat of early September. I didn't know why she had come, but I knew there was a reason.

"Mrs. Clemens," she said, "I want to ask a favor of you, and if you feel you best say no, then I'll understand. I don't know exactly how to say this because I've never been one to ask favors or to be beholden to people. But I just don't know anything else to do."

She looked so tired sitting there with dust all over her face and clothes and in her hair. She was sitting still and easy in her chair, but something in her eyes seemed to be staring out at me wild and desperate.

"Well," I said, "I'll be glad to help you if I can."

"I'd like you to take my girl."

That is all she said. I'd like you to take my girl. I rocked once more in my chair, then I answered.

"All right," I said. That was all there was to it. I didn't even think. Later, after she was gone, I thought about it and argued about it, fussed and fretted, but all along I accepted it and was glad because I had waited for a long time to have a child of my own.

But I have to admit that I was scared. Oh, I was old enough to know that nobody lives life according to the rules because, one, it's impossible, and two, there's no glory in it that way. Yet it was frightening to think what I had committed myself to. Here I was taking for my own the child of a woman I had seen only twice, a child that I had glimpsed, and that is all.

So I went over to Jessie's and I said, "Jessie, Mora Troxler knows what she's doing. There's no more cedar cutting here, and her husband is going out West. Besides, he can't keep that family alive because he's out of work so much. Mora's going with him, taking that tent and that wagon. Now what kind of life is that for a little girl, I ask you."

But Jessie just said, "Minnie Clemens, you are a downright fool."

"Listen," I said, "have you ever had a good look at Hannah? What does she look like?" And Jessie said that she had seen the child at the store with her mother and that she was small and blonde, pretty. But, being Jessie, she didn't stop there.

"Seems to me," she said, "that Mora Troxler could let that sot of a husband go his way and stay here and do housework or something and keep her own daughter in a decent way instead of pushing her off on a widow of your age."

There was nothing for me to answer except, "I reckon she has a reason for going with him and for leaving Hannah with me." Jessie had never been married so maybe she didn't know how hard it was to leave somebody you had once loved even if love was only a faint dream not quite remembered. Maybe Mora had never thought of leaving her husband any more than she would have thought of cutting off her arm. That's the way marriage is. But one thing was sure. She wanted me, Minnie Clemens, to take her daughter, and that was enough. I suppose I took Hannah on some kind of faith. I just believed that it was the thing to do.

So while my friends fussed and argued, fumed and advised, I went about the business of cleaning out the small room at the back of my house where I kept the old trunks. I had to make it fit for a daughter.

GREGORY TREMAYNE

The campus was shrouded in a gray drizzle, the cold, unsettling kind. There had been bad weather all the way from Chicago, and I was two hours late getting back. The cafeteria in the dorm was closed, so I walked over to Joe's.

Joe's was steamy and noisy, smelling of wet coats and cigarette smoke, pizza and hamburgers. I took a booth in the back and ordered a hamburger. It seemed that somehow the gray sad rain had crept right through my skin until it was inside my mind. "My mind is like a gray, gray sky," I recited idly. The waiter came and put my hamburger down before me.

It used to rain like this back in Fremond in the fall. These were what I called oatmeal cookie days because Mother always made them on days like this. Funny little Mother. She is a bit ridiculous, but then I guess that's one of a mother's rights.

It is strange that seeing Secoria Jackson in Chicago would make me think of home so much. Well, I suppose she was a pretty important woman in my life. When I was eight years old Father bought a horse for me from Terrell Jackson, and Secoria taught me to ride it. That was my very first time to have a crush. I thought she was the grandest human being on earth. There ought to be a law against meeting old loves again after you've grown up. I always thought of her as big and strong, but now she hardly comes to my shoulder.

That horse was a palomino, and I named him Lucky. Secoria always called him Lucifer, and so did everybody else except Secoria's mother. She called him Lucky like I did. I always liked Mrs. Jackson.

One time when I was at the ranch I saw a picture of a skinny little girl with long braids, and Secoria said that it was her mother. She was very solemn in the picture with her eyebrows pulled down low. Maybe it wasn't the bishop's mother who died after all, Secoria. Maybe it was just that little skinny girl with the long braids.

34

LETTER FROM GREGORY TREMAYNE
TO HIS FATHER, MOFFETT TREMAYNE,
WRITTEN NOVEMBER 4, 1960

Dear Dad,

It is midnight, and I should be studying. I can't keep my mind on political science, so I thought I would write to you. I keep thinking of you the last day or two, of you and Fremond. You see, I ran into Secoria Jackson in the Chicago airport, and she told me that her mother had died. Now I know this sounds funny, but when I got back to the campus I seemed to be seeing things differently because suddenly it was like all of Fremond rose up like a filter screen through which I had to look at the rest of the world. I am afraid that I'm not making sense in this letter, Dad, but I know you will try to understand it.

I always thought a lot of Mrs. Jackson and Secoria too. Mrs. Jackson was my Sunday school teacher for a long time. The other Jacksons I never knew as well, but they all seemed to be people that you wanted to know. Yet no matter what they seemed outside—pleasant, laughing people—taken together as a group they have lived lives that have not been easy but really, in a way, violent. And when I think of what I know of Mrs. Jackson and put that up by some of the facts that you and Sye John have told me, I realize that I never knew her at all. And somehow, Dad, I regret this. It would seem that just to understand Fremond, Texas, would not be beyond a man.

I suppose the truth is that I'm homesick. I want to be sitting there in your office again looking out the window. I want to sit in the square with Sye John and listen to him tell me about when Mrs. Jackson was a young girl. You know, Dad, there are times when I think Sye John is the wisest man I've ever known.

Well, I suppose this is enough of midnight rambling.

Your son,
Greg

MINNIE CLEMENS

She was a lovely child, Hannah was. They came to the door that first day, she and her mother, and even covered with dust from the walk into town she was like a picture. She had been crying so there were streaks of dirt on her cheeks. Mora put her hands on the child's shoulder and pushed her toward me.

"She won't cry anymore," Mora said. "She's promised me."

"Hello, Hannah," I said, thinking that I would always comfort her when she cried.

"I told her that I picked you because when I saw you at church I knowed you was a good woman," Mora said. Then she kissed the child clumsily and walked back across the lawn and down the road. Hannah stood looking after her with eyes hot and dry, clutching in her hand some flowers that she had picked beside the road, pink primroses that grow wild. Hannah and I never saw Mora Troxler again.

The first year was hard for the child. She would run away to the springs and look for her mother. But she didn't cry.

"Jessie," I would say, "if that child would only cry it out. She's too little to carry so much sorrow around inside her." Then Jessie would bluster and fuss because there was nothing we could do to help the little thing.

Hannah had been with me for eighteen months when word came from a county hospital somewhere in Arizona that Mora Troxler had died of tuberculosis. I tried to tell the child so she would understand how much her mother had loved her.

"Don't you see, Hannah," I said. "She loved you so much that she did the hardest thing of all. She gave you up because she knew she was sick and she wanted somebody to take care of you who could love you and send you to school. Somebody she knew, so you wouldn't be left with strangers. She didn't want you to be alone when the time came." But that little thing just sat on my lap stiff with grief and kept repeating, "I am alone. I am. I am."

36

Those were the fine years of my life, those years when she was growing up. She grew like a flower, tall and slender, with a face as pretty as the morning. Before I realized it, she was a young lady, smart, quiet, gentle. At her graduation from high school, she stood like a queen. Oh, I was proud to the point of bursting! But she was always lonely; she never really knew peace. I couldn't teach her to laugh, either. There are some people who never laugh easy. Yes, I'm afraid my Hannah was one of those young people to whom life is a battle, an enemy, a foe to be defeated. So it was natural that she should turn to thoughts of heaven.

It seems likely that Mora had told her about church, because even when she was small she liked to go. Then, too, Mora had come to the church to find somebody to take her child, so she must have told the girl that churches were safe places, something to be trusted. Yes, Hannah grew up loving the church. She didn't like people much, so she put all her heart into loving God.

TERRELL L. JACKSON

It was spring, and the year was 1920. I went down to Cyrus Barton's drug store to pay my bill. Mary had been reminding me for two weeks that the bill was due.

I asked Cyrus what I owed him, and he said for me to go back to the office and ask his bookkeeper, so I went to the little room at the back of the store and she was sitting there with her head over the books. Her hair was wound around her head in braids and the back of her neck was exposed. Sunlight came in from the window and seemed to gather in her hair. I thought to myself that we should thank God for the lovely things in this world and that blonde hair taking light to itself was one of them. Then I said, "Excuse me, ma'am," and she turned and looked at me. Her face was fragile and small, her eyes dark and large. I thought that I had never seen so much beauty and gentleness in any face.

"May I help you?" she asked, her voice low and even. But she blushed as she spoke, and then I realized that I must have been staring at her.

"My bill," I began. "I wanted to pay my bill."

"Your name?" she was looking down at the file on the desk, and her eyelashes were thick and dark.

"Jackson," I said. "Terrell Jackson."

She looked up quickly from the file. "You bought the Riggs place, didn't you?" She blushed again. I knew somehow that she had embarrassed herself by speaking so freely.

"Yes, I did. It joins my ranch so..." I suppose I just let my words wander off. But she had recovered her poise and was sitting quietly in her chair watching me.

"I have always been interested in the Riggs place because of the double springs."

"Oh, yes, ma'am. I'm thinking of making that into a picnic place. It's lovely there. One of the prettiest places in this countryside." All the time I was thinking that I sounded like a damn fool drummer trying to make his first sale or a high school boy trying to impress a girl.

"When my parents and I first came to Fremond we camped there at the double springs. My father chopped cedar for Mr. Riggs." She looked at me levelly. If I live to be a hundred I shall never forget her sitting there at that desk so young and so proud, challenging me with those fierce eyes. My father was a cedar chopper, Mr. Rancher, and I'm not ashamed.

On the way out I stopped and asked Cyrus the name of his new book-keeper, and he looked at me sharply, a little crossly. But he told me and all the way home I repeated to myself, Hannah, Hannah, Hannah. Forgetting that I was twenty-eight years old, a veteran, a rancher, a married man with two fine boys, with a wife who was vigorous and strong and who had a laugh that would ring against a wall.

Her name was Hannah and she was as lovely as the spring.

REVEREND STEPHEN LONGSTREET

When I was at the church there in Fremond I used to feel better on Sunday mornings to see Hannah Troxler sitting there in the choir. When a minister is young it helps if he can sometimes borrow faith from those of his flock who have the most of it. Or maybe it is courage that he borrows.

At any rate, I was proud to have a young person like Hannah, who was consumed by love for God. I was visiting with Mrs. Clemens once and remarked on the girl's deep and sincere devotion. Miss Minnie (that's what everybody called her) said to me, "Yes, Hannah loves God because He won't ever fail her. But I wonder what will happen when she fails Him. Because she will, you know. We all do."

I was young then and had the right answers. I said, "She'll learn about love then. And about forgiveness, which is love's other name."

But Miss Minnie smiled and said, "Maybe so. Maybe she will be able to forgive Him for letting her fail."

And, of course, she did fail. But as to forgiveness, I don't know whether she learned about it at all.

IV

LETTER FROM MOFFETT TREMAYNE
TO HIS SON, GREGORY, WRITTEN
NOVEMBER 6, 1960

Dear Greg,

Received your letter this morning. After reading it, I walked down to Cabot's store and sat on the bench with Sye John for a while. Told him that you thought he was a wise man and he said, "Just old, Moffett, just old."

Well, son, it seems that you are homesick. But what you are homesick for is not Fremond; it is a home that man has never known nor ever will know. It is one that he dreams about and feels must be and never stops longing for, but I have yet to meet the man who has found it. The fall of the year is a bad time for this kind of longing. Everything in nature seems to be gathering into itself all its memories and knowledge, taking back everything that has been shared with man during the spring and summer, and man sees himself the puny wanderer destined to face winter alone.

That is a lot of rhetoric for a country lawyer, but even a country lawyer finds it necessary to rely on words when he doesn't have any answers. Because I don't have any for you, Greg, nor does Sye John. So you see, son, you are becoming a man when the questions you start asking have no answers outside of what answers you make for yourself.

I am not sure what it was you wanted to hear from me about Hannah Jackson, but I can tell you something that you may find of interest. You, of course, know of my cousin Brian Tremayne who lives in Paris. Our family is very conscious of Cousin Brian, since it is not every Texas family that can boast of having produced an art critic of some reputation and scholarship. Indeed, it is a thing most unlikely. When Brian left Fremond, it was not because he was burning with desire for art and knowledge, as you may have been told, but he left because he was in love with that same Hannah Jackson. So it may well have been because of Hannah that he is what he is today, instead of a country lawyer like his father and like I am, since I took

41

his father's place when it became evident that Brian had shaken the dust of Fremond from his shoes. You remember Hannah Jackson as a Sunday school teacher. Secoria remembers her as a mother, and I as a lovely young woman possessed of a very rare sort of courage. Perhaps to Brian she was that dream of love unfulfilled that has kept him an exile and a bachelor all these years. Who knows?

I have been thinking about your request concerning a trip to Europe this summer and think it might well be the time for such a venture. I shall discuss it with your mother and see what we can do. What would you say to a deer-hunting trip on the Pedernales this Christmas?

Love,
Dad

SYE JOHN MORRISON

Moffett Tremayne came down this morning and sat with me for a spell. He had a letter from Greg, and he said the boy was feeling blue. "He in love?" I asked him.

"No," he said, "but I think he's getting ready to be."

Now I believe there's something to that. Contrary to what most folks say, I believe love comes when we're ready for it, no sooner, no later. Of course, we never realize that we *are* ready, so it's a surprise to us. But it seems to me that a man has highs and lows in his life, like an ocean has patterns of coming in and going out. So there are times when he's all primed and ready to be in love and other times when he couldn't love Venus herself. And those of us who seem to miss out on love, well, maybe it's just that when we were ready for love, love wasn't ready for us.

Take Terrell Jackson, for instance. I suppose it don't make any sense at all that he would fall in love with an eighteen-year-old girl when he was a grown man, married, with a family, just beginning to feel his strength. And yet it makes all the sense in the world. There he was, a young man to whom things had happened fast. He'd been to school, he'd been to war, he'd married a girl from the East and brought her back here, he'd had a couple of boys. Then he was back home again with his ranch prospering and people speaking well of him. With his name up for the school board and his land stretching out around him, pretty and calm. And all of a sudden he had time. Things were going well for him; his life seemed all of a piece, and he had time to think, to feel the muscles pull in his arm, to watch the seasons come round and leave and come round again. And he had time to be lonely, to find needs in him unmet, to find yearnings he never knew he had. So he was ready to be in love.

And if he could have avoided going to Cyrus Barton's drug store and seeing her there, he might soon have found himself closed up again, content within himself. But as it was, she burst on his sight like the sun in summer.

Then take Hannah herself. She had been alone for a long while. I had watched her for ten years as she growed up, and every time I saw her she had that empty look in her eyes that I had first noticed when she was a tyke whose Mother had left her.

I'll say this for Minnie Clemens, she tried as hard as ever a person could, but there's a limit to what you can do for another. You can only give the other person as much as he's willing to take. And they shared a lot, them two. But Hannah never let Minnie give her the comfort of sharing her solitude.

Yes, Hannah was ready, too. She'd grown up pretty, but just being pretty doesn't mean beaux. Besides, she wasn't the type that bowled you over, but one of them gentle beauties that creep up on you when you're not looking. She was tall and slender. So slender that it seemed like her hair, which was heavy and long and yellow, would be too heavy for her body. She wore her hair in long braids wound about her head. She had a fragile face, like a flower, with big dark eyes, brown and secret.

She was a quiet girl, shy, given to books and churchgoing. The young men may have liked to look at her, but she wasn't the type that was easy to talk with, and she didn't laugh much. When the other girls her age began to be seen around town with beaux, you still saw Hannah going to church with Miss Minnie or else walking by herself, slowly and quietly.

Then about the time of graduation Brian Tremayne noticed her. And Terrell Jackson noticed her. And, like magic, like all women, she noticed herself. She began to blossom. She was ready to be in love.

MINNIE CLEMENS

I was an old woman, a little silly and a little wistful like all old women. I suppose I was wanting another glimpse of youth. Whatever the reason, I was glad when Brian Tremayne started coming around. Hannah had been too much alone. There hadn't been enough of the things that make people sigh for their young days. There had been no picnics, no parties, no ice cream sodas at the drug store for Hannah. She'd had only her studies and her church. Yes, her dedication and devotion to her church was a marvel to everybody. Jessie was sure that she would be a missionary. And I had shocked Jessie by saying, "Not that, Jessie. I can't bear to think of the waste of all that loveliness."

Well, silly or not, I was glad when Brian Tremayne began to come around. He was a handsome, dashing boy, always laughing. The Tremaynes have always been a goodly group of men. His father, Judson, was as fine a figure as you would care to see and a good lawyer.

I should have suspected something the first time I saw Brian at church. Now going to church on Sunday morning was not the most popular thing among the young men of Brian's set. Automobiles had come to Fremond, and we had our first country club. The young people of Brian's group were usually to be found on Sunday playing tennis at the club grounds or riding around the countryside in their automobiles. So when Brian came into church one Sunday in the spring all polished and tall in his best clothes, I should have known there was a particular reason. But it took me three days to figure it out. That was when he made his next move. He drove up in front of the house with Judith Tomlinson, a little dark girl who moved quickly and laughed loudly. They came to the porch where I was sitting shelling peas picked from the garden.

"Miss Minnie," Brian began, "you know Judy, don't you?"

"Why, of course I do," I said. "Won't you young people sit down and have some iced tea?"

"We've only got a minute—" Judy began with her usual giggle.

"That sounds real nice," Brian said. He was a sharp boy, that one. He knew right away that Hannah wasn't home from her job yet. I always liked a man that could think on his toes.

"Judy just wanted to drop by," he continued, "and ask Hannah to her picnic. She's having one Friday, out at her dad's place. Going to barbecue a lamb." I wondered how he had managed to work all this out so fast because I knew that even if Judy had been planning a picnic she hadn't planned on inviting Hannah.

So we sipped our tea and chatted about flowers and gardening until Hannah came in and I went inside to cook the peas. On Friday Brian came for her looking scrubbed and grave. He helped her into the automobile as if she were china and would break. Hannah wore a new white dress with pink roses in her hair.

"Jessie," I said, for of course she had come over to see it, "that's a smart young man."

"Well, of course he is," Jessie snorted. She set a store by our Hannah, Jessie did.

TERRELL L. JACKSON

I managed to stay away from the drug store for three whole days before I threw down the work at the ranch and drove into town. It was about eleven o'clock, and I had no business at the drug store so I ordered a chocolate soda that I didn't want and shot the bull with Cyrus, all the time watching the back door to see if it would open just the tiniest crack so that I could see if she really did exist, if she was as I remembered her. I was getting ready to leave (because no man alive can keep Cyrus Barton talking for more than thirty minutes) when the door did open and she stepped out. I can still remember that. She stepped out one step, then looked up and saw me standing there and she stopped, one hand raised toward her throat. For the briefest second she stopped there, then she came on into the store, never looking at me again.

So I discovered that every day at eleven-thirty, when Cyrus went out for lunch, she minded the store. From then on it was simply a matter of planning, of being cunning, of lying to myself that I needed to see the banker or the hardware man or look for help or finding some other reason for being in town at eleven-thirty. Not that I always went in. No, I usually just passed by to catch a glimpse of her through the window. Then I noticed that there was always somebody else in there at eleven-thirty, the Tremayne boy, and the sight of the two of them, together and young, shamed me into staying away for a whole week.

Because I was not a man to lie to myself. I never had been. And when I caught myself at it, I was sick at the thought. And sick with something else too. With jealousy. So I went to the ranch for a week to help with the shearing, taking my sleeping bag, and kissing Mary goodbye on the porch of the house. We were living in town, in the old two-story house built by my father which resembled some house he had seen when he was in New Orleans and which always rose like a grotesque dream out of the Texas plain, a ridiculous house needing tall shady trees and bordered walks to make it easy, but instead resting insecure among stunted mesquite and parched grass. Mary had cautioned me about snakes and asked me to catch an armadillo for the boys, and I rushed away impatiently, running away from the house and the town and the drug store and young Tremayne and my wife and boys and myself. And away from that memory of yellow hair taking to itself all the light that was in the sky.

SYE JOHN MORRISON

I was thirty-two years old when I lost my leg. I was off in East Texas lumbering, and like any maimed creature looking for a dark cool corner in which to hide, back I came to what had always been home to me, dragging with me my peg. Because somehow I didn't mind the eyes of Fremond looking on my peg. I guess because I knew that at least some of those eyes had seen me whole. But I should have known that a man with a peg leg is what he is, no matter where he goes.

What is a man with a peg leg? Here in Fremond he's the watcher, the talker, the bench sitter, the checker player. Once you've got a peg leg you're not going to do much traveling, just from the boarding house to the store to the lumberyard to the post office to the cafe to the bench. Especially if you ain't got no family nor land. And each time that leg pounds against the earth it's another mark in the circle you're drawing, the circle of the routes you travel in your daily round of living. And inside that circle is all the world you're going to know. Add to that the fact of living eighty-odd years watching that world—there you have an old man with a peg leg.

A man with a peg leg lives through his eyes. He watches life parade by in the faces that pass his bench, sorting out the threads of each person's secrets, storing up what he can of fact and truth, and growing old. Just like all the people who are whole. Growing old.

By the time I was forty I had lived with the peg long enough to have my world enclosed. I knew the pattern the hours took passing across the main street of Fremond where I lived my life and kept my watch. When something altered in that pattern of time, I felt it in my bones. And lots of things made sense to me before others even thought of them.

Like Terrell Jackson and his Hannah. Now I knew about *that* even before Terrell himself was sure, and why? Because he altered the pattern of time along the main street which was my given world to watch. I began to see him pass along the street on some sort of business every morning

49

about eleven-thirty. Now ranchers don't come into town at regular hours. They come when they can grab a moment or when the needs are pressing. And this is usually early in the morning or towards evening, not in the very heart of the working day. So when Terrell began walking down my street every day at the same time, I noticed it. And before too many days I knew why, simply by watching his head turn once every day. Only once and always in the same direction. Yessir, if there's one thing a peg leg is, he's a watcher.

So I saw what was happening to Terrell, but I didn't know what he was going to do about it.

Then he altered my time again. Just as I was getting used to him coming along every day about the same time, he quit coming at all. Went out on the ranch for a week. And I knew he had faced up to it and that when he came back, he would have made up his mind to something.

Yes, I could see what was happening to Terrell and also to Brian Tremayne. Brian and I, we used to play checkers while he was waiting for eleven-thirty to come. He tried to teach me to play chess, but I was stubborn even then and wouldn't learn. And Brian talked to me about the girl a little.

"She's so gentle, Johnny," he would say. "She's not like anybody I've ever known."

I told him about that first time I saw her when she rode in on the wagon, and the boy looked at me all solemn and said, "I'm going to make her proud of me if it's the last thing I do."

The boy changed that summer, growing more quiet and solemn, talking seriously of how he was going to study law at the university and of what he would do when he came back to Fremond to practice with his dad. I suppose it's only fair for me to admit that I kind of hated to see him leaving his youth and becoming a man. He'd always been a laughing kind of boy.

Well, Sye John the peg leg could see what was happening to the menfolk, but he durn sure couldn't see a thing in Hannah. She moved down his street like she always had, slowly and quietly and at the right time. There was only one slight difference. People began to talk about how pretty she was.

TERRELL L. JACKSON

Shearing sheep is hard physical work. The hours are long, your hands are busy. You pull every muscle in your body at least one more time than it is accustomed to, so you fall aching into your sleeping bag at night and awaken in the morning stiff and sore. You speak Spanish all day to your help and you holler and swear at the sheep. Shearing is a busy masculine time tinged with the smell of singed flesh. Yet a man can think a lot when he's out shearing.

My land has been more than a livelihood to me. It's been a love and a comfort. I do not lie to myself that it is beautiful land in the strictest sense of the word, but there is beauty for me simply in the knowledge of it, in the fact that I've ridden over it, that I've watched it season after season, year after year, learned to recognize the outcroppings of rocks, the draws with their turns and twists, the lines of mesquites. It is dry land, brown and parched, but in the early mornings the air is cool and crisp with a sharp edge and the land rolls away misty under the pale sky and the edges of the hills are purple in the distance. Yes, there is beauty in it. It has been a love and a comfort.

I was glad for a week of shearing on the ranch. It gave me a chance to talk to myself, to be honest. By the end of the week, I knew what I had to do, and I was determined to do it. That gentle young girl in the drug store, that lovely voice that moved across my mind like a fever—those were things I had no right to, things to be avoided. Because I was never a man to hide, to connive. If I could have walked up to her proudly in front of everybody and said, "Miss Hannah, I think you are a gift from God," then I would have done it and gladly. But I was not a man to lie and cheat, to betray promises already made and make promises that I could never keep. There's not a lot a man can know in this world, but he can try to know himself. At least that's how it seemed to me that week when I wrestled sheep in the day and my conscience at night.

That week I gained some sense of myself and my world. I saw my land and what there was for me to do with it. I saw Mary and the boys and remembered how I had married her in Virginia when we were two kids and carried her back here to this land of dust and sand. I saw the land through her eyes and realized that she was brave and lonely here where there were no orderly rows of green nor gentle ways such as she had always known. And I thought of my sons, one quiet and shy and the other still a baby. At the end of the week I knew who and where I was. Hannah had become a lovely dream from which I had awakened, a lovely dream fast fading.

MINNIE CLEMENS

I would never have gone to the Fourth of July picnic if it had not been that Hannah wouldn't go without me. I was eighty years old and the machinery had begun to run down. Now I'm not complaining, mind you. Not in the least. I never was one to expect to stay young forever. I had had more than my share of good days and if things were beginning to tire me now, well, that was all part of the pattern and I didn't mind it. God had been good to me. I had only asked for enough days to see Hannah grown and safe. And that He had given me, for here she was a young lady able to care for herself. And now there was Brian too. Yes, God had been good to me.

The day was hot before the sun had been an hour in the sky. We bounced along the road in Brian's automobile with the sky above us like a shiny metal disk. Hannah carried a covered box in her lap because all the women had to bring a lunch for two to be auctioned off. The lunches were wrapped in a distinctive manner so that the menfolk could bid for them; and the man that bought your lunch, he it was that you were to eat with. We had fixed our boxes early that morning. Hannah had insisted upon putting them inside a big box so that Brian couldn't see them. She wanted him to guess which was hers, I suppose. Well, he was a smart boy. He should be able to do that.

I suppose that all Fourth of July picnics are alike. The schoolgrounds were crowded with people talking and visiting and with children running. Hannah went off to work awhile in the church booth where the ladies were selling lemonade. Brian helped me over to the shade at the edge of the schoolyard where certain other people like myself, old and wishing a little that they had stayed home in the shade of their front porch, were sitting and talking. Then Brian went his way, and I sat there watching the picnic unfold before me. By lunchtime my eyes were full of color and people and hot Texas sun. My ears were pounding with noise and music, laughter and voices. A picnic is a good place to get your senses full of all the things that make up this world, the only world we've got. And let me tell you that this world isn't a bad one at all. For all our complaining, we do all right.

The auctioning went fast with laughter and joking, the way it always had and the way it should. When Hannah's box was held up Brian guessed it right away, but the boy made a nice gesture. He didn't bid on it but waited to buy mine, just like a Tremayne because they've always been gentlemen. Hannah's box was bought by someone else, by Terrell Jackson. I believe that he bought it not knowing who it belonged to, because when Hannah stood to walk over to him I saw his face go white and the muscle along his jaw tighten. Then Hannah's hand, which was clutching her skirt, trembled ever so slightly. That was all that happened, but somehow I knew that fortune had not been kind to those two people that day at that picnic. Life is lots of things, but it's never simple.

SYE JOHN MORRISON

A man can figure all he wants to and plan things out to where every loose end is all tied up in a pretty bow, but that don't make one damn bit of difference. It just don't matter at all.

Ole Terrell, he came back from that week at the ranch and he didn't come to town anymore, he didn't go to the drug store, he didn't look at the girl. No, he just dug his toes in and fought with all he had. And that's considerable because he ain't ever been what I would call weak. He was doing good too, beginning to relax a bit and feel that the danger was nearly over, when along came that blamed picnic and like some bird dog he spotted that lunch basket and bought it, not knowing that she had packed it and that he would be honor bound to eat with her under the trees.

And Hannah too. She was a woman, wasn't she? So of course she had known why he came by every day at eleven-thirty to look into the window. And she had known too when he stopped coming and why. So it wasn't easy for her to sit there on the grass beside him and try to talk to him. But sit there they did, like two people in a dream, helpless and a little dazzled.

TERRELL L. JACKSON

God forgive the man who ever feels like he's winning, for as sure as the sun rises in the east, he's not. The best we can hope for, endowed as we are with only a modicum of wit and no understanding, is to keep even, to stay alive, to hold our heads just above the surface. I was feeling strong, the master of myself, logic's victorious knight. And, as inevitably as darkness follows light, I landed on my face, tripped by something as innocent as a picnic.

I had not feared the picnic because I felt myself to be over the hurdle. Terrell, you old dog, I thought, you've been playing the fool's game. Lusting after your youth in the form of that young girl. Hell, man, I said, you ain't old enough for that sort of fancy yet. Because every man both hates and prizes the poet in him, the romantic, the dreamer. So I went to the picnic secure in my own sense of law and facts. The seasons come round each after the other and never do they fail. That is all a man needs to know, I said. That time is motion and change. Yes, I was armed that Fourth of July, only it wasn't enough.

For they held up a box tied with a yellow ribbon in which were caught three white daisies. And, laughing at the foolishness and comfort of rituals, I purchased the box, not knowing that I was also purchasing time. Yes, time *is* motion and change and I had purchased time with Hannah under the trees where we were bound by the foolishness and comfort of old rituals to sit and talk together. And that time, my logic and my weapon, moved around us wiping away all my strength and reasoning.

The grass was not abundant and green but parched and brown so that it crackled under her skirts when she moved. The shadows were not heavy and dark but sun-sprinkled shadows, the shade of stunted mesquites and hardy live-oak. We sat down and I felt old and useless, young and frightened, sad and happy. What did I say? Something meaningless, like It's hot today, isn't it? And she said something equally foolish like We need rain, don't we? But her eyes were shadowed and searching. For she looked at me, straight at me, in spite of the fact that she was afraid too. And her eyes seemed to have no bottom to them but stretched endlessly away into paths more dark and secret and majestic than I had ever imagined.

"I guess young Tremayne got his signals crossed," I began lamely, trying to laugh, trying to remember who I was and what I was.

"No." Her voice was low and sure. "He's eating with Aunt Minnie. I know he planned it that way."

And then, because I knew she prized honesty and because I knew also that I could not plan what to say but must simply speak, I said, "I didn't, you know. It wasn't planned."

And she answered as honestly, "No. I know that you didn't."

Why is it that often when a man quits fighting and just accepts, he finds that it's like a gift? That was what it was, that hour under the trees. A gift. She sat across from me and we talked of the double springs and of the land around us. We smiled together, even laughed. And we were silent too. But it was all like a fine and wonderful gift. Because we had accepted all the forces that had moved us to that time as well as the forces that would grow out of it. Yet for that hour they were forgotten through their very acceptance, so we were easy together, calm and free.

Then the hour came to its end. I felt the gears of the clock begin to move when she said gaily as she glanced across the schoolyard, "Look! Brian is making a dandelion chain." I could hear the movement then, and I was back with my old sickness, sick, both of shame and jealousy.

"I guess you'll marry him," I said. But it wasn't the easy, teasing way I had wanted to say it, the way any other man at the picnic could have said it. And she would have answered as lightly, as teasingly as they. Instead she looked at me again, firmly and quietly, but searching too. "No," she said finally. "I don't think so."

That was all there was to it. An hour under the shade at the edge of the schoolyard.

Picnics are a foolish and illogical phenomenon, a random and distorted pattern. Like the ways of a man.

BRIAN TREMAYNE

I have celebrated many Fourth of Julys in Paris. This year I shall, no doubt, go to the garden party at the American embassy. For some unknown reason, the embassy feels that it is necessary to give a garden party each year to comfort the homesick exiles on this, the most American of days. Well, I'll go and happily spend the time conversing of French affairs and drinking French wine. I shall most likely leave more homesick than when I arrived.

Paris has been good to me and I love her. She is my mistress to whom I shall remain faithful until death. But, my Paris, I am allowed one day of the year, am I not, to think of that other love left behind?

You see, my Beauty, I might never have seen you had it not been for that earlier love to whom I foolishly and faithfully drink a toast every Fourth of July. You understand, of course, that I am faithful in all that I do, even in remembering.

There is actually little relationship between a garden party at the embassy and a picnic in Fremond, Texas. Except that they both occur on the Fourth of July. So my attendance at the garden party is only a little gesture, one of those small ceremonies on which I've based my rather comfortable life and without which I would be lost. It's my way of nodding gently to my youth.

I wonder if they still have the picnics at the schoolyard. I would imagine so, with the heat shimmering up from the ground and a dusty haze hanging over the yard from all the feet moving across the packed dirt where no grass would ever grow. Imagine that, Paris. It is hard to grow grass in Texas.

Yes, it was like another world. I was young and sure of myself that last Fourth of July with my old love. And very much in love. In love with life, youth, Texas, and my lovely Hannah. A little in love with Miss Minnie too, I suppose. We rode out to the picnic in Dad's car, the three of us. I have never felt more triumphant than I did that day, knowing that all the people of Fremond would see us together and that they would somehow know that Hannah belonged to me. Which goes to show just how foolish it is to be young. Only the young can assume that because they love, they are loved in return.

It was in every way a memorable Fourth of July. Miss Minnie and I ate our lunch in the shade, and I even made a dandelion chain while Hannah was across the yard with Terrell Jackson. She would have turned heads here on your boulevards, Paris, she was so lovely that day. As she walked across the yard to where Miss Minnie and I were sitting, you could see the heads swinging to watch her. She moved like a queen in her yellow dress with her hair soft around her face.

That evening we sat on the steps at her house and watched the stars come out. It may be hard to grow grass in Texas, but, my God, the sky! There is nothing like that wide shimmering night sky. I could smell the perfume of her hair as we sat there.

"Hannah, do you know how much you mean—" I began.

"Shhh!" she said, putting her fingers on my lips. They were cool, with the same sweet fragrance of her hair. "Don't talk, Brian. Just watch the stars."

Then, as I was leaving, she said, "Brian, you're a fine person. I'm sure that I shall always be proud to know you." She went quickly inside, leaving me there alone with the night brilliant and shimmering around me.

So I didn't tell her that I loved her that night as I had planned. No, it was about a month before I told her, and by then I was already beginning to know that I had lost.

I drink a toast to her every Fourth of July too. To Hannah Jackson, who ever lives in my memory as a young girl in a yellow dress, beautiful, mystical, and just out of reach.

MINNIE CLEMENS

After that picnic on the Fourth of July, I knew why Hannah had grown pale and silent, why she ate very little, and why she prayed for such long periods alone in her room. I also knew why she would walk through the house at night and sit on the steps watching the stars parade across the sky. Oh yes, I knew. But there was nothing I could do. I couldn't help at all. I could only love her and sorrow for her helplessness. And hope that Time would be kind to her.

Then there came the morning when I awoke and it seemed as though I was under water and watching the world through the cool green while the lines of familiar objects danced and swam around me. When I tried to raise my arm it was heavy and moved slowly, floated up through that same green, wavering detachment. So I knew that Time and I were soon to be one. Once again my Hannah would be left alone. Like Mora Troxler I must leave her; I could not help her any longer. But, also like Mora Troxler, when I left my Hannah, I would be leaving behind all the love of which I was capable.

REVEREND STEPHEN LONGSTREET

It was the middle of August when Miss Minnie fell ill. Hannah called for me early one morning in the Tremayne boy's car. We drove out to the house together silently, for although I was younger then and a little more optimistic, a little firmer in belief, I was already feeling myself helpless in times of sickness and death.

And we both knew that Miss Minnie would die. She was old and frail. Only a few months before, in the spring, she had said to me, "When you have lived with Time as long as I have—and that is Death's other name, Preacher—you learn to be both patient and resigned. You learn not to quibble and argue with him. I guess you sort of compromise, losing something by it, no doubt, but gaining too. Because you gain the right to be not afraid of him anymore. There's nothing he can do to you that you don't expect or can't accept. He can't scare you any longer. And that's something, you know. To outlive fear."

But she lingered longer than we expected. For ten days she was very ill, and on the eleventh day, before dawn when the air was cool and still, she raised Hannah's hand to her lips, kissed it, and died.

All through those long days Hannah had been as strong as faith itself. She had stayed close and cared for Miss Minnie with all the strength and tenderness that any human being could summon. I had noticed that twice a day she slipped away to the church, where she knelt upon the cool floor and pressed her head to the smooth wood of the pew. Once I saw her shoulders shaking as she knelt there, but when she arose her eyes were dry and her face bore no sign of tears. Everyone asked, "How is Hannah standing up under this?" And I answered, "She is a wonderful girl, strong and fine. And she knows how to pray."

It wasn't until Miss Minnie was gone that she fell across the bed and wept.

Why is it that the man of God, who should deal with human gains, finds himself always confronted by the sorrowing spectacle of human loss?

61

TERRELL L. JACKSON

When I heard that Miss Minnie was ill, I wanted nothing so much as to go to Hannah, to help her, to stand by her. But I had fought this all out with myself. Except for that one unforgettable, impossible, wonderful hour at the picnic I had avoided so much as catching a glimpse of her. When I heard Miss Minnie was ill, I began to plan a trip to the ranch house. Mary was going to Virginia with the boys for their annual vacation, leaving on the train the next morning. There was no reason for me to stay in town where Hannah was, where I could feel her pain turning like a knife inside me. Every street seemed to lead to that little house at the edge of town where she struggled brave and alone. So alone. I had never seen anyone so very alone.

I put Mary and the boys on the train to Virginia and went straight from the station to the ranch. The house at the ranch was dusty and close-smelling. Nobody had lived there for years. But within a day or two it was my home, lived in and comfortable. I even managed to grow friends with the silence. And I thought about Hannah and why I had felt the impact of her so deeply. She was beautiful, yes, but that didn't matter. Lots of people and lots of things are beautiful. No, it wasn't beauty. It was something about her that was untouched. She seemed almost like a child, a lonely sad child who needed to be taught to see things, to feel things, to feel life and love. She needed to be sheltered and guided gently past all her fears, past all the rocks that shatter delicate bark to some safe harbor of understanding where she could see that just to be alive was a reward in itself. I wanted to teach her to take joy in building life, in making order, in watching the years come round. I wanted to share with her what I had here on my land. And I wanted to give her tenderness, love, and tell her that she wasn't alone. That I would never leave her or forsake her, that she had a friend to care for her.

But I was resigned to the fact that those things were Brian's to do for her. In time I wouldn't even feel the need. If I could be strong, time would pass and I wouldn't feel the need. But why, I kept asking myself, does he have to be so young? He's too young to know what she is.

The ranch house had been deserted since I had returned from the war and dismissed the foreman. There was only a trail leading down to it and one path coming from the creek. Nobody ever came that way, so I was alone at the house. I had no way of knowing when Miss Minnie died.

MOFFETT TREMAYNE

I was only a kid, but I still remember when Aunt Sophia came running across the yard from her house and up to the kitchen. She was crying, dabbing at her eyes with her apron. Mother and Aunt Sophia were more like sisters than my father and Uncle Judson were like brothers, although they had never known each other until they had married the brothers and moved next door.

"Clara," Aunt Sophia said, weeping, "he's so young." And I knew she must mean Brian, since he was her only child, and I was sure she didn't mean Uncle Judson. Mother was very calm, as usual. "Tell me, Sophia. What happened?"

"He wants to ask her to marry him. Hannah Troxler. He came in today from the funeral and sat in a chair in the living room for a long time. Then Judson came home and he asked Judson to give him the ring his grandmother had left for him to present to his fiancée. Well, Judson almost perished on the spot. They're such babies, Clara."

"Was Judson sharp with him, Sophia?" Mother knew Uncle Judson's temper.

"He tried to reason with him. He talked about how long it would be before Brian was a lawyer and could afford a wife."

"Didn't that do any good?" Mother was a practical woman.

To her, there was no questioning the practical.

"Brian said that he just wanted to be engaged to her. That he couldn't bear to leave for school without knowing that she was waiting for him, that he was becoming a lawyer for her. Then Judson got mad and they argued and Judson stormed out of the house." Aunt Sophia began to cry in earnest. "Oh, Clara, I did such a silly thing. After Judson left I went upstairs to the safe and got the ring and gave it to him."

Mother put her arms around Aunt Sophia. "There, there, dear. It will be all right. Judson will forgive you. It will be all right."

It was some time before I could piece together and understand the events of the next two weeks. The next thing I remember is Aunt Sophia crying again, this time because Brian was leaving for Brown University instead of the State University at Austin where they had planned for him to go. But Brian was dead set on going a long way from home and Uncle Judson had gotten him into this school in the East and we all went down to the train station to say goodbye. Brian looked pale and serious as the train left. The ring had been returned to the safe by this time. I don't suppose Brian ever asked for it again. At any rate, when Greg was born Uncle Judson brought it over in a velvet box and gave it to Emmaline. Some day, I suppose, Greg will give it to the girl he has chosen and never know it once was offered to Hannah Jackson.

I was a grown man before I got the facts from Aunt Sophia as to what happened the day of Miss Minnie's funeral. It seems that Brian took the ring from Aunt Sophia and went to Hannah's house that evening about nine o'clock. But Hannah wasn't home. He waited all night on the front steps, but she didn't come. When he went back the next evening, she refused him with great finality.

SYE JOHN MORRISON

I was sitting on the bench. It must have been about noontime because I was still working then and was only on the bench during the hot part of the day when we laid off at the yard. Brian came up to me and sat down slowly. He put his long legs out in front of him and just sat there for a while.

"I came to say goodbye," he said. "I'm going up East to school, Johnny." For some durn reason that kid always called me Johnny.

"Well, Brian," I said, "Guess you can teach them old boys up there a few things about the fine art of checkers."

"You take care, Johnny," he said as he got up to leave.

"I'll be expecting you back to play me a game about Christmas time."

He was awful serious that day, in the way only the young can be. "Won't be back then, Johnny. I think my business here in Fremond is over."

"What about your girl?" Now I could have guessed, but I knew that he wanted to tell me.

"She doesn't want me. She won't ever want me or need me."

"Well, boy, this here's a mighty big world and there's lots of women in it."

He smiled then. "Yes, it's a big world. So I shouldn't miss this one little corner of it, should I? Goodbye, Johnny. You're a good man but a lousy checker player."

And he was gone. He was a fine boy, that Brian. I should have learned to play chess just to please him.

TERRELL L. JACKSON

It was early night, the time when the light is spattered faintly against the darkness in such a way that day is only a memory and night is only a promise. I was lying on the bed smoking and listening to the crickets out by the pond. I think I sensed a human presence before I actually heard the knock because I sat up and listened. Then the knock came, a gentle tapping.

When I opened the door she was there, dust on her clothes, her hair falling in strands from her braids, tear streaks on her face. She must have run most of the way from the double springs along the creek and up the path to the ranch house.

"Oh, Terrell," she cried, her voice low and whimpering like a little child's. "She died. She died."

Then I was reaching out to her and she was safe in my arms, clutching my shirt and sobbing against me.

"She left me too. She left me."

Decisions are made quickly sometimes. At least the important ones. I suppose I made mine in the split second it took for me to see her standing there and to reach out to her. From then on there was no turning back.

When I awoke the next morning, I knew that whatever else might happen in the world, I would never leave her, that she belonged to me and I would not deny or hide that fact, just as I would not forsake her. I looked at her asleep on the pillow with all her beautiful hair spread across the white linen. Whatever pain and suffering followed that moment, Hannah, both our own and others, could be balanced, I think, by that brief time of joy, that contentment of knowing you were mine, that you were my love.

SECORIA JACKSON

Mother's timing was always good. Or maybe she simply chose the right people. Or was it a combination of both? That must have been it. It would have taken both in order to assure so much success, so many victories. Hannah of the Indomitable Will and the Incredible Luck.

It was really too bad that Father drank so much, wasn't it, Hannah? Otherwise I might never have known as much as I did. But he had to have somebody to talk to, somebody who would listen to the story of his life. His poor, wasted, confused, struggling life. Well, there's nothing wrong with that. We all need a listener. But Mark wouldn't listen, Timothy was afraid to, you didn't dare, so that left only me. I listened and I learned. I learned about you and what you did, what you were.

It wasn't too smart of Father to fall in love with you when he was married. That wasn't wise at all. But he could have lived through it, he could have recovered, Mother, if you had let him. Because he always was a fighter.

He told me how he fought against it. When he was drunk and crying, he told me in bits and pieces how he ran away from you. After all, he was the older man, married, settled. And you were the young innocent. Isn't it nice that we can always distinguish the villain and the victim? And who could accuse you, when you were so young and pure and innocent? Devoted only to God and the woman who had raised you.

But Father also told me something else. He told me how you came to him at the ranch. You came to *him*, Hannah. When he was running away, when he had never spoken a word to you of love or tenderness. Yes, you were alone, you were frightened, you were sad and young. But there were other people. There was that Tremayne boy. Father said that he wanted to marry you. But you chose Terrell, and you came of your own free will to the ranch. He couldn't run any farther than that. He was cornered there in the house and you came to him there, knowing who he was and what he was. Yes, it was a combination of timing and of choosing the right people.

SYE JOHN MORRISON

What Terrell Jackson did has been discussed so many times in this town that I guess once more won't hurt. Of course, you'll find as many accounts of what happened as you will people. But I believe the facts are nigh to this.

About three days after the funeral Hannah left Fremond to visit somebody up near Wichita Falls. Now she said she was going to see a cousin of her mother's. Since nobody in Fremond knew anything at all about her folks, we accepted this. But I believe what really happened was that Terrell Jackson sent her to stay with some friends of his. She was gone until the first of the year.

In the meantime, Terrell took a train to Virginia. Before he left he instructed Judson Tremayne to sell his house here in town. Now it seems that he went to Virginia and asked his wife for a divorce. They must have settled it all between them because we never saw his wife or two boys again. I did hear once that his wife had married again and lived in Pennsylvania, and I remember that he used to go see the boys once a year. At least he did for a while, but by the time Mark was in school, he had stopped that. Be that as it may, I do know that he gave his wife a goodly sum of money. He gave her all that he had from the sale of the house and all the money he had inherited from his father. The only things he kept were his ranch and enough capital for running it one year.

Terrell Jackson had been a wealthy man. And he was to be again. But for a time he was a working rancher, struggling to make his place pay. That was part of the price that he paid for Hannah Troxler.

When he returned from Virginia, he set about fixing up the ranch house so that when he brought Hannah home, there would be a place for them. Now the town still hadn't figured out what was happening. Or at least they hadn't put two and two together, because when Terrell went to

Wichita Falls in January and returned with Hannah, married to her, you have never seen such a commotion.

Terrell Jackson was an honest man and a brave one. I have to say that for him. They were both brave.

MARY LANIER JACKSON KERR

Do you want to know what I felt that day when Terrell told me, what I honestly and truly felt? Relief, that's all. Just one large flood of relief. Of course, that was only for a moment, then all the other things begin to ring in me—hurt, injured pride, loss, fear, regret, anger. All of it. But for one pristine second, it was nothing but pure relief.

It would be easy to say that I never should have married Terrell and let it go at that. Unfortunately few things are that simple. When I first met Terrell I was just a child. He had come to Virginia with his father to visit their cousins. Anna, his cousin, was my best friend, so it was natural that I should be asked over to play with the wild boy cousin from Texas. We were children, yes, but even then I knew that I had not met anybody quite like him. He was different from my brothers, my friends, from anybody. He came back to Virginia to visit twice while we were growing up. Then, when he was twenty-one and I was nineteen, came the fourth visit. How can I describe what he was like to the young girl that I was? Like a whirlwind, I think. He swept into my life and everything else seemed to vanish. He was strong, self-sufficient, confident. Beside him all the men I knew seemed pale, weak, posing. He told me of his ranch, of Texas, of his plans. I was captured by the word pictures he built; it was just one more step to seeing myself, like a pioneer woman, beside him in Texas helping to make his dreams come true.

So I decided to marry Terrell before he had even noticed me, I think. And it wasn't all because of him. Partially it was the idea I had of myself bringing order to a raw new land. And Terrell was lonely. His father was dead; he had no one. So when I cried and swore that I could not bear for him to leave me, he was touched. From there on it was easy. A month later we were married in the garden of my home.

How could I have known what life I had chosen for myself? I had never been farther west than Atlanta. The land burst on my sight like the

71

blaze of sun at noonday. I sat by the train window transfixed by the sheer nothingness of it. The land stretched away on every side until it touched the sky. That was all there was, the brown parched land stretching evenly to touch the edges of that pale blue bowl of a sky. It hurt my eyes, the bold bare reaches of color, the blue blazing and endless, the sand brown, parched, and endless. This, then, was my new home where I was to carve out a Virginia life of order and tranquility.

How could I have known what kind of man I had chosen? I had never met a man like this one before. He was not a man of words and books like my father but a man of doing. He was a man who sweated and swore. His hands had broken nails and callused palms. To this man a horse was not a bloodline but a working partner. He was not a man easily possessed.

And whatever a woman may say, that is what she desires: to possess. I did. I still do. Women are the realists of this world. We want only those things that are sure and knowable, land under our feet, a roof over our heads, china in the cupboard. We want a man whose soul we can hold in our hands.

Yes, it was relief I felt first. That is more than a woman can bear, a home which grates against her eyes, a man whom she can never understand.

GREGORY TREMAYNE

When I first came to Iowa as a green freshman I discovered rather quickly that the most interesting thing about me to the majority of my new friends was the fact that I was a Texan. "This is Greg Tremayne," a person would say, introducing me. "He's from Texas." Not that I minded. Hell, no. I was even a little proud.

In the last three years I've gotten used to being the Texan. I actually haven't noticed it much. Until last night. A bunch of us were sitting around the dorm playing cards, and some new guy asked me where I came from. Tony, my roommate, answered for me. "Texas," he said.

Then I did a funny thing. *"Fremond,* Texas," I corrected.

"What the hell." Tony shrugged. "Texas is Texas."

Maybe so. But I come from Fremond, Texas. One certain place. Maybe Fremond is Texas and maybe Texas is the United States and maybe the United States is the world. Only I don't know yet. Not for sure. I don't even know what Fremond is.

I can describe it, yes. It's a small place, about six thousand people. It has one main street, a long one. I can remember that when I was a kid this street still had wooden sidewalks. I used to walk on them barefooted.

The town is sort of built in a circle and in the center and at the end of the main street is the church. It's a square, dark granite building, sturdy and weathered, with a squat ugly steeple. Sye John always said that steeple proved that religion around Fremond was lacking in imagination. Perhaps. But it isn't lacking in power. The church is to Fremond what a hub is to a wheel. It is located on a block in the center of town and out from that block the streets radiate like spokes. It seems that the founding fathers (among them my great-great-great-grandfather Tremayne) built a church before they built homes. And the rest of the town grew up around and in reference to that church.

When a person is born in Fremond he can no more escape that ugly building than he can escape breathing. Not that everybody there goes to church nor are all Protestants. I don't mean that. I simply mean that the church is a force in Fremond. It is always there, omnipresent, behind everything that happens, coloring every thought, every reaction, every deed. It is our interpreter, our judge, our admonisher, our ruler.

It really makes life pretty simple, the church does. It gives Fremond a way of balancing itself that's easy for a person to understand. There are two kinds of people: those in the church and those out of it. There are two kinds of places: those approved of by the church and those disapproved. There are two kinds of activities: those in accordance with the church and those not. A strong clear measure like that makes it easy for a person to know where he stands with respect to sinning.

Naturally the church is not as powerful as it once was. The people aren't as pleased with simple solutions anymore, I guess. But when my dad was a kid, it still ruled with an iron hand. As a matter of fact, Mrs. Jackson—Hannah—was kicked out of it because she transgressed the rules. It seemed that Terrell was already married when she decided to marry him, and to the church there was only one term for such a thing—adultery. So they withdrew membership from her. That used to be the practice in some small southern towns. If you got caught doing something wrong, the church could withdraw membership from you. Of course, it didn't matter if you had been sinning for years if you kept it quiet. But once the sin was public you had to pay for it. Morris Boynton, the ginner, had a "lady friend" (as Sye John put it) in Austin for years. Went up twice a week to see her. Yet he was head layman at the church. Because he was discreet, I guess—a successful way of sinning.

Sye John had a theory about successful sinning. He thought you could sin openly and blatantly, then repent even more openly and blatantly. "If there's anything this world loves," the old man would say, "it's somebody who admits he bears the mark of Cain."

I suppose that is what Mrs. Jackson did, for by the time I remember her she was one of the leaders of the church and, therefore, of the town. So I guess she had sinned publicly, then repented even more publicly. But somehow that doesn't seem to fit the picture I've always had of her. She seemed so proud. And truly righteous. Most of the women who were active in the church merely struck me as noisy figures with admonishing fingers which they were constantly shaking in someone's face. But Mrs. Jackson was quiet about her religion, like it was a private thing. That kind of faith was a rare thing in Fremond.

Well, there's probably more to the story of Hannah Jackson and the church than I'll ever know. Underneath the simple dividing line of that square drab building, that clear outward pattern of right and wrong, the threads of Fremond are as tangled as a knot of yarn and nothing or nobody is really one or the other but a part of all.

REVEREND STEPHEN LONGSTREET

The news about Hannah Troxler and Terrell Jackson exploded over my parish like a skyrocket. I'll never forget it. Maude came bursting into my study at the church, her face a battleground where outrage and excitement contended. "How could she do a thing like that?" Maude kept asking, her voice colored by those dual emotions.

Myself, I was young and didn't know much about people or churches or life or anything. But I knew lots of words. Yes, I bartered quite a bit in words like Love, Faith, Duty, Sin. Everything in black and white. Black words like sin; white words like love. It all seemed so simple and clear. It's the easiest thing in this world to deal in words, but it doesn't mean one thing. You can send words out over the heads of your people every Sunday, but that doesn't have anything to do with their living.

Poor deluded creatures who believe that living is words, who recognize life only when it is printed on a page or spoken in the air. How intolerant we are when the rhythm of living does not coincide with the rhythm of our sacred, our holy, our abstract and exalted words.

But as I said, I was too young and simple in those days. Like the rest of Fremond, I was thoroughly shocked that Hannah could have coveted and taken another woman's husband. That went against my black and white words. Now I was aware that such things happened, but they didn't usually happen in Fremond and certainly not among the more faithful of my church members. I think that is what puzzled me most. How had this happened to Hannah? And how was she going to live with it? For although I was young, I had already learned to sort out my parishioners. I had learned that few who enter the doors of a church do so for the sheer love of God. Not that it matters. The church is big enough to embrace many reasons for the coming. But I felt a special concern for those who seemed to be seeking constantly for the meeting in the burning bush. That was how Hannah had always been, looking for God with a faith like flame.

So how did I fit all this together?

Well, I didn't have much time to try. A short while after Maude left the study, Morris Boynton came by.

"Morning, Preacher," he said.

"Morning, Morris. What's new at the gin?"

"Nothing. Nothing at all."

"What's on your mind, Morris?"

"Nothing much. Just thought we ought to talk about the Sunday school program."

I knew what was coming then. It was definitely not the habit of Morris Boynton to leave the gin in mid-morning to discuss Sunday school.

"Anything wrong with the program, Morris?"

"No, Preacher. It's a fine program. Just wouldn't want to see it damaged in any way. We got to be awfully careful, Preacher. Careful about who we've got in there teaching and things like that."

"You served on the selection committee, Morris. You know all the teachers."

Morris took out a handkerchief and wiped his red sweaty face.

"That's right, Preacher," he said, putting the handkerchief back in this pocket, "only I didn't know everything about some of those people. At least not all that I know now."

"What are you getting at, Morris?" I was determined to make him say it. At least I can give myself credit for that.

"Hannah Troxler," he said.

So there it was in my lap.

"You're going to have to do something, Preacher," Morris said, leaning his red face toward me.

"What would you suggest, Morris? The only way I would know to help somebody who hasn't asked for aid is to pray for him."

Morris pulled a cigar from the pocket of his jacket and pointed toward me with the end of it. "Don't know much about things like that, Preacher," he said. "All I know is that we can't have a woman like that teaching our kids."

It seemed like praying about it wasn't going to be enough.

"I'll talk to her, Morris," I said.

He got up and started out.

"You do that, Preacher. It's not that I'm trying to pass judgment or anything, but her being here with those kids Sunday morning could cause a lot of trouble. There are lots of women in this town who'd be offended by something like that."

I thought of his wife with her sharp hard face. "I'll talk to Hannah," I said.

"Yes sir, Preacher, you do just that. After all, the church has to take a stand in matters like this."

He left then, his cigar clenched between his teeth, unlit. Morris would never have been disrespectful enough to smoke in the church building.

I sat there for a moment, then bowed my head and prayed. "Oh God," I prayed, "give me the strength to walk in Thy paths and to keep Thy laws." Then I got up and walked over to the house. Maude was in the kitchen. I opened the door and called to her. "Don't wait lunch," I said. "I'm going out to the ranch to see Hannah."

TERRELL L. JACKSON

I brought Hannah home in winter. The sky was heavy and leaden and the mesquites, which could look like delicate lace in the spring, were bare and black. The ranch house looked lonely and deserted when we drove up before it. I cursed myself inwardly for not having one of the Mexicans light a lamp or build a fire for us. But she clutched my arm tightly and said in her soft way, "It's wonderful to be home, Terrell." And, though I searched her eyes for any sign of pain or fear or regret, I saw only happiness. And love.

We had been home three days when the preacher came. I saw him coming up the lane, so I went into the house where Hannah was preparing lunch. She was standing at the window looking out at the lane, her shoulders tensed. When she heard me enter, she turned and smiled at me. "I'm glad I have enough food to set another place," she said.

It's a funny thing, but I've never been able to dislike Preacher Longstreet. I think I even threatened to kill him once, but I never disliked him. And when Hannah died, he was the only one I could think of that I wanted at the funeral. Which makes absolutely no sense whatever considering the role he had played in our lives. I remember that I felt a little sorry for him that day. He was a young man with his first pastorate and his was not an easy task. But he came right to the point.

"No, thank you, Hannah," he responded to her luncheon invitation. "Maude will be waiting lunch for me at home. I just came out to talk with you about your plans."

"I'm afraid I don't know what you mean." Hannah spoke very clearly and precisely. I had moved behind her chair just in case she needed help. But it was probably I who needed the closeness of her.

"Well," he continued, drawing a deep breath, "you're the elected teacher of the ten-year-old girls' Sunday school class. However, since you've been away Mrs. Jordan has taken that class."

"Yes," Hannah answered calmly. "I hope it hasn't been an imposition on Mrs. Jordan."

"No," Longstreet said. He looked right at her too. I have to give him credit for that. "In fact," he continued, "I think it might be best if you resigned the position and let Mrs. Jordan continue."

There was a silence while Hannah regarded him silently across the room, her gaze level and steady. His eyes dropped first.

"I see," she said in her low even voice. "Is that all, Reverend Longstreet?"

"Yes," he said weakly. Something seemed to have gone out of him. "You're welcome at church, of course, but under the circumstances I don't see how a position of leadership is possible," he finished with a helpless sort of gesture.

It's a funny thing, but I wasn't angry with Longstreet even then. Because I didn't need his church. I had my wife and my ranch. And I suppose there was something more. I didn't want Hannah to need his church either.

"You sure you wouldn't like some lunch?" I asked.

"No," he answered. "I have to be going."

After he was gone she turned to me, her eyes fierce and stern with the effort to hold back tears. "Lunch will be getting cold," she said.

So I sat down to my lunch thinking that she would soon get over her hurt feelings. I knew, too, that the town would eventually forget its outrage. In time it would all be forgotten. And time was what we had. We could stand any little affront to our dignity because we had time. Time together. That was what I had wanted, and that was what we had.

Which all goes to show how little I knew about this lovely girl I had married. How very little I knew and understood! To myself I said, That's that with Hannah and her church! and began to eat my lunch.

NELLIE BARTON

Sure, I'd known Hannah when she worked in my brother's drug store, but I had never thought I'd have to take sides against her in anything. She worked well. She was quiet. You never heard bad talk about her like you did some others. Everybody down at the church thought she was a good Christian girl. You listen to me! You got to watch them "good Christian girls" like you got to watch all of them. Man crazy, every last one of them!

Still and all, nothing would have come of it except talk if she hadn't tried to flaunt herself in our faces. Nobody can expect people to sit back and take that. People can do whatever they blessed well please just as long as they keep to themselves, but don't let them come hanging around respectable people. Or trying to force themselves in some place where their kind of living is a disgrace.

That's exactly what Hannah did by coming back to church. We thought sure she wouldn't have the nerve to show her face there again. And when she did, well, we saw our duty and we done it. It's as simple as that. The whole business has been talked and retalked in this town a hundred or more times as to whether what we did was right or wrong. I admit that it got a little out of hand, but I'd do the same thing over again. After all, how could we sit there every Sunday and watch her and Terrell Jackson walk in like they owned the world? Wouldn't that be a way of condoning their sinfulness? What kind of example would that set for the young people? No, there was only one right action, I don't care what anybody says!

We had all heard that Brother Longstreet had been out to the ranch on Saturday to tell Hannah that her usefulness to the church was over, so we figured that was the end of it. I, for one, had washed my hands of the whole business. Then Sunday morning as we were singing the Doxology, I heard a rustling in the back of the church. Old Mrs. Crozier must have had one of her seizures, I thought, turning round to look. But it wasn't that. Oh no. It was Hannah and Terrell Jackson walking in just as big as you please.

81

Hannah was dressed up in a new outfit that must have cost a pretty penny, and Terrell was handing her into the pew. They were acting like nothing was wrong, like everybody in the church hadn't stopped singing in order to stare. Only Ben Simms, the song leader, was left singing with his voice sounding like a hollow reed. Then Terrell handed Hannah the songbook and they both joined in with Ben, the three voices carrying the whole song for about four measures before the rest of us began to recover.

Now right there is where I think Preacher Longstreet done wrong. He should have prevented them coming in the first place. But instead he went right ahead and preached his sermon like nothing had happened. Then came time for the invitational hymn at the end of the service. Of course, I thought to myself, that's why they came. She wants to ask forgiveness of the church so nobody could blame her for anything to her face. As much as the thought of such hypocrisy irked me, I had to admit that it was smart thinking.

But I was wrong again. Because they just sat there like they were as good as everybody else and had nothing to repent. When the service was over, they made their way out like it was a normal Sunday morning. Like everybody wasn't standing back, staring at them. They shook the preacher's hand and walked outside. And then—well!—I just wish you could have seen the reaction inside that church! It's one thing to sin; it's another thing to flaunt your evildoing in the faces of God-fearing people.

Still and all, I wouldn't have done anything if a group of people hadn't come to my house Sunday afternoon. Everybody was upset about that morning, I can tell you! So finally Myra Cabot and I were more or less nominated to go to the preacher and tell him what certain of the church members felt should be done. Somebody had to. It was plain that he wasn't going to do anything.

He was in his study when we got to the church.

"We'll come right to the point, Preacher," I said. "We feel that the church should censure Hannah Jackson."

Longstreet blinked at us from behind his glasses. He was a little fellow, always reading books and blinking. Personally I never had much use for these little men who always have a book under their arms. They're always weak. Always trying to look at both sides and usually missing the picture.

"On what grounds?" he asked.

"Well, really!" Myra said.

"Open and flagrant adultery," I answered.

Longstreet leaned forward and clasped his hands together on the desk.

"Miss Barton," he began, "don't you know the church was created for sinners?"

"Repentant sinners," I answered, "which Hannah obviously is not."

"What would you require of her, Miss Barton? That she give up her marriage now that it is already contracted?"

"Well, really!" Myra said.

"I'd require a public confession," I said. "Before the church."

"She's given up her place of leadership. It seems to me that is enough."

"She can't be allowed to come here again like she did today with the two of them as proud as peacocks. It's a slap in the face of the church. Either she makes her position of repentance clear or else we should deny communion to her."

Longstreet took off his glasses and blinked a few times. "I suppose now is the time for me to ask the classic question of whether or not you are willing to cast the first stone," he said.

"I'm willing to stand for what's right," I said.

"You remember, of course, that in the Bible the casting of the first stone was to go to one who was without sin." The preacher spoke slowly like he was tired.

"I'm willing to stand for what's right," I said again.

We sat for a few moments in silence with the preacher looking across at us and now and then running his hand over his eyes. Then he put his glasses back on and said, "I'm sorry, ladies, but I think I've made my position clear. I feel the church does not require further action in this matter."

"The church is God's institution and has to take a stand, Brother Longstreet," I said.

"I cannot be a party to any action against Hannah Jackson," he said.

We gathered up our gloves and purses and got up to leave. At the door I turned to him. "Don't think you've heard the last of this, Preacher. The church outlasts preachers, you know." And with that, we left.

When we got outside, Myra turned to me, her face flushed with anger from the way he had treated us. "Well, really!" Myra said.

REVEREND STEPHEN LONGSTREET

I have spent many an hour reconstructing the Hannah Jackson affair in my mind. Throughout my entire ministry, in church after church, town after town, there would come a time when, late at night, alone in my study, I would put down my book and relive each step. And now that I am old and retired, I have nothing to do but relive bits of my life, both failures and successes. Sometimes they become confused in my mind.

Fremond was a failure, there is no doubt about that. My first church too. That was a pretty frightening thing for a young man, to fail with his first pastorate.

I suppose there were many reasons for the failure, the main one being fear. Oh, I was brave enough when faced with the self-righteous pressure of Miss Nellie Barton and that foolish Myra Cabot. But it was another thing when the Board of Stewards came to me. It was a little harder to summon up nerve. I was still holding out, probably as much from stubbornness as from principle. "No," I said firmly, "we will not withdraw church membership from Hannah Jackson." That was at the board meeting on Thursday.

You know, sometimes I think it would be best if a minister did not have to depend upon the church for his livelihood. A man might be able to act with more bravery if his job were not going to be affected.

When I got home, I found Maude crying on the bed. She had her dream of a nice church in a county seat town. One with a decent parsonage in which to bring up the kids. And, to be honest, so did I.

"Do you know what's going to happen, Steve?" she asked tearfully. "You're going to be removed from this pastorate by request of the church, that's what. Your whole career is going to be ruined because of that—that woman."

I comforted her as best I could. But I wasn't too happy over that prospect myself. Unfortunately a man's own dreams of glory often become entangled with his ideas of right and wrong.

Then Maude tried being logical. "You're destroying this church, Steve," she said. "Splitting it into two factions. Is Hannah Jackson really worth this?"

And so I found a pattern of reasoning. All week I kept asking myself, shouldn't I, as the pastor, follow the wishes of the church? Is it right the church should suffer this discord, hostility, and confusion on account of one sinful woman? Isn't it better that the one suffer for the sake of the whole? After all, the members were not asking more than what the church was actually entitled to.

Because I felt that they had a right to deny her membership. She had sinned willfully and knowingly. My church gathered itself around those holy words Thou Shalt Not. Hannah knew this as well as anybody. And yet she had taken another woman's husband. It was written Thou Shalt Not, Hannah. Thou Shalt Not.

That was how I talked to myself. And gradually, I suppose, I came to a decision. Although I didn't realize it until my hand was forced the next Sunday.

SYE JOHN MORRISON

Don't go to church very often. Just a matter of principle with me. Of course, like all people, I'm always willing to ditch my principles when curiosity gets the best of me.

Take that Sunday when they kicked Hannah Jackson out of the church. Now all that week I'd been giving them church people hell. Like a damn bunch of buzzards, I said. Found a weak spot on somebody so they're looking for a chance to polish her off. It's a downright disgrace, I said. Then I heard a rumor that there was going to be some action that Sunday night at church. Back in those days, one sermon a week wasn't enough. We had two Sunday services, one in the morning and one at night. I guess they chose the night service because there are things in this world that are easier to do when it's dark. At any rate, the word went around town that Sunday night was when it would be. So what did I do? I dressed in my black suit, tied on the only tie I got, and went down there to watch. I was above joining in the pecking, yessir, but I wasn't above watching.

Now just to set the record straight, I never cared much for Hannah Jackson. Don't really know why. Probably because a talker like me always envies them what can keep their business to themselves. Those of us who are always having to reach out to people, we kinda resent them what's strong enough to stand alone. At any rate, I didn't feel no obligation to Hannah as a person. I was only a spectator, curious about all the goings-on.

The church was packed. Almost everybody in town was there. I never will forget Longstreet's face when he came out on that platform and saw all them people. He must have known right then that something was up, because Fremond was like any other town. People here don't take to church-going on Sunday night. Usually Longstreet would have been greeted by a small knot of his most devout worshipers, so when he saw that crowded room, he stopped for a moment, his face pale and stricken. He was in a hard spot for a young man. For any man, I guess. I ain't got nothing but pity for them what's forced to sit in judgment.

Of course everybody there knew that Longstreet had flatly said no to the request that Hannah be excluded from the church. What Longstreet must have guessed when he saw all them people was that the members were going to bring it up anyway. All during the sermon Morris Boynton kept looking at his notes. As head of the board, it was his duty to open the meeting.

Now like I said, I never cared much for Hannah Jackson, but I ain't cruel, neither. I took one look at that church full of people and then I said to myself, I hope to God she don't come. Not that they looked so mean or anything. It was just the goddamn curiosity! Sure, I was guilty too. That didn't make it any prettier.

But she came. And for the first time since her marriage, she came alone. They were living out on the ranch, so we didn't see much of them in town. Terrell had no way of knowing what was in store for Hannah that night. It seems that he had gone over to Lampasas to see about hiring some men, thinking that she would be all right. Thinking that by now people would have seen that they were prepared to stand together against whatever the town could give them. Right there may have been the worst mistake of Terrell's life. Because Hannah had to be alone again when she had thought that she would never be alone anymore.

She came in with that chin high as usual. She took a seat midways down on the right side. Then she fastened all her attention on the preacher. It was a hard night for Longstreet. I don't remember what he tried to preach about, for, like everybody else, I wasn't paying the least bit of attention. I was just waiting for the sermon to be over.

And finally it was. Longstreet was raising his hands to pronounce the benediction when Morris Boynton's voice came out of the congregation.

"Just a minute, Preacher. I have something I want to bring before the church."

Longstreet stood there gripping the sides of the pulpit. Everybody leaned forward, kind of holding their breath. The way I see it, there was two things Longstreet could have done. He could have refused Boynton the right to speak. If he had done this, I believe Morris would have yielded. After all, it wasn't exactly the right way to handle church business and ole Morris wasn't nearly as sure of himself as Longstreet may have thought.

There was a lot of people watching who knew Morris Boynton pretty durn well.

The preacher stood there for a full minute, his knuckles going first red, then white, on the edges of that pulpit. Then he yielded the floor to Boynton. Ole Morris stood up there with his fat face red and sweating. He kept wiping it with his handkerchief while he read his statement. I don't remember exactly how it went but the meaning of it was clear enough. It mentioned the fact that the church covenant forbade adultery. Miss Hannah Troxler (Morris didn't even use her married name) had publicly broken this sacred law by marrying a divorced man. Therefore the church had no choice except to demand her public confession and repentance that night in front of the entire body. If she refused, it must deny her membership in the congregation.

When Boynton sat down every eye turned toward Hannah, who was sitting stiffly, still looking at the minister. I won't ever forget that face. It was as white as death; her eyes looked as though they had been burned into it. The skin was stretched tight over the bones until it looked more like a mask than a face. She was young, you know. And serious about church.

All the curious waiting eyes swung around to Longstreet, who was standing at the pulpit again. His hands were clutching the edges just like before. When he tried to speak, he had trouble with his voice. He looked at Hannah with as pleading a look as I have ever seen and then he said, "Mrs. Jackson, is it your desire to make such a public confession?"

She stared at him for a moment out of that mask-face. Then ever so slowly the mask crumbled away and the face of a child stared out, a child who has had a bad dream and still believes in it when he is awake. She half rose from her seat, crouching like an animal who is trying to escape from a blow. She never took her eyes from the preacher's face.

"Confess?" she asked at last. "Confess what? What is it you want me to say?" She was standing now. And her voice had risen to include a note of pleading. She clutched the pew in front of her and spoke to the preacher in that wild demanding tone. "What do you want me to say?"

Longstreet's eyes moved over the church rapidly and for a moment I thought that he was going to order everybody out. Contempt was all you could see in his face. Then he turned back to the girl, his voice under control now.

"Confess that you sinned in your marriage and ask for the forgiveness of this church," he said.

"How can you ask that?" she said softly, only to him. When he did not meet her eyes, she turned to the church and asked piteously, "How can you ask that?" Then, seeing all the downcast heads and averted eyes, she slowly straightened and walked out into the aisle. Near the end she stumbled once and had to grasp the end of a pew to keep from falling. No one moved to help her. No one even dared look at her. The only sound in the church was the sound of her broken weeping.

Longstreet stood for a moment after she was gone. His face was colorless and tired. So was his voice.

"I am sure that Mrs. Jackson will accept the decision of the church to exclude her from its active membership." He paused, the muscles working in his jaw. "You may all go home now," he said. And turning, he left the pulpit without benediction, without prayer.

Slowly we gathered ourselves together. Slowly we arose from the pews and went out into the night. Nobody spoke. Most of us turned our faces away from any other that chanced near us. Even the curious get their fill.

TERRELL L. JACKSON

When Hannah was ill—shortly before her death—I was sitting in the room with her. We had been sitting silently for an hour or so. Then I noticed her hand fluttering in some sort of gesture as though she were beckoning me closer. I leaned over her and she whispered to me, "You never could understand my faith, could you?" I held her hand in mine and answered truthfully, "No."

I knew that she shouldn't try to speak, that even that effort exhausted what little strength was left to her. But there was something else I wanted to ask. "Was it worth it, Hannah?" She looked at me for a long time, but she did not answer. Finally she withdrew her hand and turned her head away.

Over the years I have spent a great deal of time trying to understand just how Hannah believed, what her God was like. It seems to me that He must have been something of an almighty, stern, terrifying father. And her belief like to that of a child in a dreaded but loved parent. Her religion was a Puritan one, founded on denial, sacrifice, and fear. Mainly on fear. It was a narrow religion, simple, provincial, unloving, unforgiving. It was a southern religion, repressive and fierce. I'm not sure that Hannah believed in a heaven, but she was certain that there was a hell. She was willing to do anything, make any sacrifice, in order to escape this place of torment. Once I asked her lightly, "What is this hell of yours like, Hannah? Does it have fire and brimstone?" She answered seriously, "It is a place where you are separated from God." I think this meant to her a place where she would dwell alone with nobody to protect her or care for her. Like a child in a hostile world beyond her comprehension.

Actually I knew the tenets of her faith. It was the sort of Protestant religion that Fremond, like other southern towns, gave lip service to and pretended to mold itself in accordance with. But most of the people adjusted the doctrine to fit their own human needs. Only a few, a very few, dared to do what Hannah did. Only a few took upon themselves the task of sincerely trying to embody the will of God. Only a few dared attempt to be the perfect child of this vengeful Father.

Yes, I had known that Hannah was serious about her church when I married her. But I had thought it was the simple piousness of a sheltered child: a habit, not a conviction. I didn't understand at all.

It is useless to speculate whether things would have been different had I not gone to Lampasas the night of the scene at the church. Sooner or later it would have happened anyway. Sooner or later I would have become Hannah's guilt and she would have become mine. Because Hannah loved two things: her strange, implacable God and me, an ordinary human being. There will always be guilt when love is divided, when the loved objects are two things that not only do not contain one another but which often seem to exclude one another.

And me. I loved two things also. It was that other love that took me away that Sunday, that sent me into Lampasas leaving her alone, when she thought that she would never be alone again. I left her alone for one last time, the time that would plunge her into loneliness so deeply that never again could I comfort her.

That Sunday I had awakened before daylight. I was standing on the front porch watching the sun come up slowly, hesitantly, gently pushing back the mist. Gradually out of the blending purple and gray and pink I could see my land rising up from the shadows and stretching out before me. I had been a long time away from it. A long time waiting and planning for Hannah, arranging for the welfare of Mary and the boys, fixing up the ranch house. I had been a long time in the service of my other love. Now I could see the land rising around me, feel it reaching out to the sky, to the edge of my sight, and I knew that I was ready to work again, *must* work again. I went back into the house and bent down over the sleeping Hannah. Her lovely hair was spread over the pillow. Gently I pushed it away from her cheek and, aching with love for her, I touched the smooth soft skin, knelt to kiss the purple-shadowed eyes.

"Hannah," I spoke softly, "wake up."

She moved drowsily, smiled a little, then reached out to me. She pulled me down against her so that my cheek rested on hers.

"Must you always get up so early?" she murmured sleepily.

"I've got to go to Lampasas," I said. "It's important."

"It's Sunday," she said. "You don't need to work on Sunday."

"Sunday is the best day for locating good hands," I answered. "Everybody will be in town lounging against the buildings or playing checkers on the courthouse square."

"Come back to bed," she said. "It's still early."

But I resisted the gentle tugging of her arms, the smoothness of her cheek.

"I've got work to do, honey," I whispered against her hair.

So I went away to Lampasas in the service of my second love, to gather the men I needed to keep my land secure. And by my going and leaving her alone the guilt entered in, never to leave again.

It was late when I drove up in front of the house; yet I somehow had expected a light to be on. I stumbled into the house, cursing, and lit a lamp. The light traveled across the wall until it revealed the shadow of her head. She was sitting in the big chair, her back straight, not touching the chair. One yellow braid had come undone and her hair hung ragged around her face.

"Hannah," I said, bending close to her, holding the lamp near her face, "what is it? What happened?"

She looked at me and it was all written there in her face. Only I didn't know how to read it then. All that had happened, that would happen, that had been said, that would be said, that we had done, that we would do, it was all in that face with its tear stains, with the eyes separate and alone and empty. It was written in each line of that set and suffering face. And there was more. All that she was spoke out. All of her pride, her fear, her searching, her love, her hate. All the things that made her: the deep quiet places, the storms, the frightened child, the strong woman—they all looked out at me through those dark and bottomless eyes. If I could have read your face, Hannah, and known what you were, what our life would be, could I still have gathered you to me? Would I have still taken your incoherent, your mute and comfortless sorrow into my heart and life and made it my own? I think so. I think I would still have taken it, even if I had known.

It was almost daybreak before Hannah slept. Then I left the house quietly and drove into town. The first light was beginning to show in the sky when I reached Morris Boynton's house. I had to knock several times before his wife answered the door.

"What do you want?" she asked.

"Tell Morris I'm here to see him."

"He's sleeping."

"Tell him I'm here, Mrs. Boynton."

I suppose she could tell by my face that if he didn't come out, I was coming in, so she went after him. A few minutes later he came to the door, hastily tucking his shirt into his pants.

"You ain't looking for trouble, are you, Terrell?" he asked. I didn't even answer. I just grabbed him with one hand and hit him with the other. Mrs. Boynton screamed when he hit the porch. I waited for him to get up, but he simply lay there looking up at me and saying over and over, "Now, Terrell. Now, Terrell."

"You sorry sonofabitch," I said.

It was a short distance to Longstreet's house. When I knocked he answered the door himself. He looked as though he had not been to bed. He was fully clothed and his face was drawn and tired. I looked at him standing there, and suddenly all the fury was gone. I could not beat back time if I personally whipped every man in that town. I could not erase what had happened or remove my own absence or physically force myself a place in the moment of her humiliation. Nor could I bloody and mutilate the face of that guilt which had come to dwell with us.

Neither the preacher nor I spoke. We simply stood and looked at each other. Finally I turned and walked away.

Hannah was still sleeping when I got back to the ranch.

VI

SYE JOHN MORRISON

Terrell Jackson tried hard to make it up to Hannah. Maybe he tried too hard. But what was done, was done, and nothing he could do would change it. It was just a matter of learning to live with it. Besides, it weren't only the Jacksons what had to learn to live with that Sunday night. It was all of Fremond.

Now it didn't take long for everybody to know that Terrell had paid a visit to Morris Boynton. And there was those of us who were kind of tickled by that. I always sort of wished that I had seen ole Morris getting his.

There was them that were scared too. Many a man in this town kept an eye on his door for a few days. There were some men who were friends of Terrell's that had been at the church that night, silent as stones. They weren't relishing having to explain their actions to him. But Terrell must of got it all out of his system with that visit to Morris because he didn't come to town for a couple of weeks after that.

And during that two weeks Fremond drew its breath and began to relax, began to forget. It was time for forgetting. Sin had entered the town, been called by its right name, and punished. Now we could forget it. People began talking about other things.

The Jacksons just seemed to withdraw. Terrell didn't come into town much, only when the ranch needs were pressing. We never saw Hannah at all. When Terrell came in, he was quick about his business, not talking much. Which everybody understood. For he was having to work hard now. He didn't have any money to fall back on, so it was up to him to make the ranch pay. And he was sure as hell going to do it. You could tell that by looking at him. He was leaner now, tanner. He wore dusty work clothes and his hands were harder. He had more weather marks around his eyes and fewer words to waste. Ranching ain't ever easy, don't guess. I suppose Terrell didn't have too much time to brood about what had happened. His land was demanding lots of work and lots of thought.

I used to watch him going about town busy with his work, and I wondered what Hannah was doing, how she was filling her time. Because all she'd ever had since she was a little tyke was the church. It was all she had wanted. And now she didn't have that. She didn't have no friends, either. She had Terrell, true enough, but she was sharing him. I wondered about her, young as she was, alone as much as she was.

Terrell must have thought about that too. Because he bought her a present. Yessir, he bought her a fine thoroughbred horse, which seemed a strange sort of present to most of us.

Now we're ranching country round here. We're used to horses; they're part of our life. Nothing special about a horse. 'Course, most of our horses are quarter horses, sturdy little work animals. But this horse that Terrell got for Hannah, he was the finest animal we had ever seen around this town. I remember the day that horse came in on the train.

It was early in the morning when I saw Terrell and his hired hand come into town. They had a horse trailer behind the truck, and they drove down by the railroad station. When the 6:10 train pulled in, Terrell walked alongside it till he came to a railroad car where a man was standing looking out the door. They talked a moment, then they led the horse out. Terrell stood in the railroad yard holding the reins while all the men within seeing distance gathered around. He was some animal, that horse was. Black as the night and shining in the morning sun. Glistening like silk. His legs were slender and he kept prancing and pawing at the ground, arching his neck.

"Lord god, that's an animal for you," somebody breathed. "What you going to do with him, Terrell?" another man asked. "He ain't no work animal, that's for sure."

Terrell was watching that horse, his eyes full of pride. "He's for Hannah," he said. "I got him for her."

The men got sort of quiet then. They didn't ask no more questions. But they stood around watching while he and his hand got the horse into that trailer. Gathered into a knot, they stood looking after the truck and trailer as Terrell headed out of town.

"That was some horse," a man finally said. "Proud son of a bitch."

"What's a woman gonna do with a horse like that?" asked a boy. But nobody bothered to answer him. They just stood watching that truck go down the road.

GREGORY TREMAYNE

I was down at the railroad station when they unloaded Hannah's black horse. My dad had come into my room that morning and awakened me while it was still dark outside.

"Get up, son," he said. "I want you to see something." I got up and dressed in the dark, wondering what there could possibly be to see that would cause my father to let me get up in the night. I went downstairs with my shoes in my hand, knowing instinctively that my mother was still asleep, not even aware that Dad and I were up. Dad was in the kitchen drinking coffee.

"What is it, Dad? What are we going to see?"

"Something," he answered, smiling at me. My dad was a quiet man. He worked in the bank and wore glasses. "You want some coffee?" he asked. I nodded wonderingly. Mother never let me drink coffee. He poured me a cup and I drank a bit of it. It scalded my throat, bringing tears to my eyes. Dad finished his coffee and put the cup down. "Come on, Gregory," he said, "before your mother wakes." And we slipped out the back door into the early morning.

The town looked different as we walked along the street toward the railroad station. Something about the gray misty light changed it all. I had never seen it in the early morning before. "Where are we going?" I asked.

"There's something coming in on the train that I want you to see," he said. And we walked on in silence while the still houses loomed out of the mist as though they were floating, while our shoes grew wet and dark from the dew.

We walked into the station yard just as the train pulled in. The sun was up by now and there were a few people around the station. Sye John was there, and some of the men who worked for the railroad. There were others too. Men in from the ranches to pick up packages, equipment, items coming in on the train. Dad and I walked along beside the train until we caught sight of Terrell Jackson talking to a man in one of the cars. Dad stopped then and put his hand on my shoulder. They let down the doorway to the car; then they led the horse out. He came out slowly, looking all around. The sun, just coming up, showered its red light all over him as he picked his way delicately, proudly, out of that railroad car. I had never seen anything like him.

"There he is, son," Dad said happily. "There he is." But I couldn't even speak. My eyes, my throat, all of me seemed filled with the beauty of that horse, with the longing to possess him. Terrell led him out into the yard and all the men began to gather around, all of them staring just as we were. Finally I said to my father, "Who does he belong to, Dad?" dreading to hear, fearing it, but longing, hoping that possibly he might, he just might...

"He's Hannah Jackson's horse," my father said shatteringly, not even noticing the hope in my voice.

Terrell led him away before I could so much as touch him. Dad and I watched them drive away with the horse, then we started back home.

When we got to the house, Mother was up. And angry. "Whatever got into you, Moffett," she fussed at Father, "taking that child out in the chill morning air just to see some ole horse."

"It wasn't some ole horse, Emmaline," Father answered patiently. "That horse cost so much money that Terrell Jackson had to borrow from the bank in order to pay for it."

"Borrow money?" Mother gasped. She was a practical and frugal woman. "You mean he borrowed money to buy a *horse?* Whatever for?" Then, with dawning suspicion that caused her to narrow her eyes, for she was also a straitlaced and righteous woman, "It isn't a race horse, is it?"

"No," Dad answered, watching her slyly from behind his glasses. "It's a thoroughbred saddle horse. One of the best you can buy," he said.

"But what on earth could he want with a horse like that?" asked Mother, still puzzled by the enormous idea of someone borrowing money to buy an animal.

"He got it for his wife, for Hannah," Dad said with the slightest trace of amusement in his eyes.

Mother didn't say a word; she just looked at Father, shocked. Then she slowly shook her head in amazement.

I never coveted anything in all my young life like I did that horse. His name was Rajah. I still remember.

TERRELL L. JACKSON

God only knows what made me think of buying that horse. I just wanted to give her something. And I wanted it to be something that we could share, that would make us closer. So I thought of the horse. If she had a horse, I thought, we could ride together in the evenings. We could ride out over the ranch and look at the land. She could learn it as I knew it, learn to love it. If we could just share the ranch, I thought, it would give her something. Something to help her, to keep her from being lonely. Something new to love.

Yes, I was foolish. And a little desperate, wanting so much to make her happy, to fill her life. Wanting also to get rid of my guilt, for if she loved the land too, it would be all right.

I went down to the bank and borrowed the money to buy Rajah, knowing full well that Hannah had never ridden a horse, yet somehow hoping that the beauty, the magnificence, of such an animal would win her, would make her *want* to ride him. William Tremayne who lent me the money said, "That's a funny thing for you to be buying, Terrell."

And I said, "It's not for me, it's for Hannah."

"It's still a funny thing for you to be buying," he said. But he gave me the money and I brought the horse home to her.

Manuel turned him loose in the small corral so that when I brought Hannah out of the house, the first sight she had was of him prancing and running in the yard, tossing his head, getting the feel of the ground again after his long trip on the train.

"There's your surprise, Hannah," I said, pointing to him. I was very proud. He looked just the way he should, magnificent, proud, spirited. She didn't say a word, only looked at me, her eyes wide and startled. Then slowly she walked out to the fence. She stood there for a long time looking at him, watching him. Manuel and I were grinning and proud. Then she turned to me and asked in that deceptively soft voice, "Why, Terrell? Why did you buy him?"

98

I didn't understand. God help me for being an ignorant fool, but I still thought she was going to be pleased. "For you," I said. "For you to learn to ride. So we can ride together over the ranch. He'll be something for you to have to fill the time," I said.

She looked at me for a long time, her eyes deep and secret, searching my face. Then she looked back at the horse. "I don't want him, Terrell," she said. She turned and walked into the house.

SECORIA JACKSON

I have to laugh when I think of Terrell being so foolish as to make Mother a present of Rajah. A *horse,* of all things! For Hannah! What a foolish, clumsy, funny, dear, transparent gesture. Oh, I can just imagine it all— Terrell leading her out to the corral. So sorry I fouled you up with your religion, dear. Here. I'm going to let you share mine.

Only Hannah wasn't buying. She wasn't trading her dream of heaven for a measly little ranch. Not her.

No, all Hannah wanted was to be back in her church again. And she wanted to be back with her God. Somehow the two were twisted together in her mind. And Terrell wanted Hannah and the ranch and somehow these got twisted together in his mind. Then Mark, Tim, and I came along, all wanting things, everything becoming more twisted. And none of us got what we wanted except maybe Hannah. I think probably she did, and perhaps that is what I can't forgive her—the fact that she got what she wanted. Or maybe I just can't forgive her the price we all had to pay to see that she did.

Well, I guess Rajah was one of the mistakes with which Terrell paid. God, he was a gorgeous animal! I can remember how beautiful he was, and how I cried when he was sold. When I was small, not even in school, I asked Daddy to give him to me and he said, "He belongs to your mother. Ask her." So I went to Mother and asked, "Mother, may I please have Rajah?"

And she said, "Rajah? You mean that horse?" she shrugged. "It's all right with me," she said. So he became my first horse.

It was a good thing that he finally was given to me. Neither Terrell nor Hannah could stand the sight of him, nor could they let him go. A matter of pride, I suppose. If anybody should understand about the strange maneuverings of human pride, I should. Whatever the reasons, Rajah had been more or less ignored for all the years he had been on the ranch except for the loving care of Manuel. And together Manuel and I made him into the best horse in three counties.

Mother used to worry about me. "She'll be a tomboy," she said. "She'll never outgrow those horses." But I did. Oh yes, I outgrew them just as I seem to outgrow everything. And sometimes I wish to God that I never had.

Yes, it's funny that Dad thought of giving Mother that horse. It is also pathetic and tender and touching. It's funny that Mother never accepted the gift. It is also pathetic and tender and touching. One of those outrageous, ridiculous, destroying mistakes that build us into a lopsided world where we stand looking out, confused to find ourselves the captive of our own errors.

I rode lots of horses as a youngster, but Rajah was the finest.

TERRELL L. JACKSON

Hannah walked back into the house leaving me stunned and angry and hurt. Yes, I was hurt that she had rejected that damn horse, hurt that she had rejected my plans and hopes. We stood looking after her, Manuel and I. Finally he moved closer to me.

"Señor?" he asked. We had known each other a long time. We didn't have to waste words.

"She's not interested in him," I said curtly, and began to walk away.

Manuel hesitated for a moment, then followed me a few steps before asking, "We send him back then?"

"No," I said, never pausing. "We don't send him back."

He let his breath out slowly. "Manuel will care for him," he said. Then he turned noiselessly and went back to the horse.

Yes, I sulked like a hurt child until Hannah was touched and contrite. That night she lay in my arms and cried.

"I only wanted us to use him to share the ranch," I said.

She wept softly against me. "I didn't intend to hurt you, Terrell. I love you." So I began to recover and be forgiving and loving. Finally she lay quiet against me, no longer crying. "Terrell?" she said when I thought she was already asleep.

"Yes?"

"I want something we can share too. I want a baby." And there it was. My answer. Something so easy, so natural, that I couldn't think of it myself. A baby.

A baby could be everything, I thought. It will be a son, of course. Born of our love, sheltered and protected by it. A son to grow up here at the ranch, for the ranch to belong to someday. It would be the perfect way of sharing for Hannah and me.

"We'll have a son, Hannah," I said.

"Soon?" she asked.

"As soon as you like." Then, reconciled, happy together, we slept.

It must have been near dawn when I awoke to the sound of the back door being opened. I got up and went to the window. Hannah was going down the path to the double springs. Yes, I knew that she went down there often. And I knew that she went there to pray. But why tonight? I wondered. Why now?

It was two years before I found the answer. It was because she couldn't trust me to give her a son. She had to ask him of her God.

VII

REVEREND STEPHEN LONGSTREET

I should have left Fremond after the incident with Hannah Jackson. Now it seems to me that I only stayed there in order to punish myself. If that is so—and I'm not sure of anything at this age in life—I picked a worthy expiation, for I could never look at that town, that church, those people, with the same innocent faith again. Not that I hated or blamed them, or even that I hated or blamed myself. It was simply the constant need to relive it, to wonder about it, to question. Sometimes I think that I couldn't leave Fremond until Hannah herself set me free from it. A romantic notion, no doubt, but one with an ounce of truth in it.

Actually, I saw very little of either of the Jacksons for two years after Hannah's expulsion from the church. Terrell was busy on the ranch and Hannah had withdrawn inside the safety of Terrell's love. She rarely came into town. Why should she? She had never had many friends there. Her only interest had been in the church. Denied that, there was nothing in Fremond for her.

And the times I saw Terrell he seemed well, prospering even. I remember that he seemed to give out such an air of strength. I envied him that. He seemed so sure of what he was, where he was going. The two of them have built a strong world for themselves, I thought. Even without God, I added, enjoying the irony, enjoying the fact that this was something new for me to ponder. Could Hannah have found enough in human love to satisfy her? Was there enough in that for a person? Yes, there were plenty of questions to trouble a young preacher in Fremond. He didn't need to go looking elsewhere.

For two years I was free of Hannah and Terrell Jackson, but I couldn't leave Fremond. Then suddenly I was confronted by them again. And after that time I felt free to leave the town.

It was a little over two years after the Sunday we had expelled her when Hannah came to my study. It was early on a Sunday morning. I was in my study, working on the sermon, for it had always been my practice to be in the church by sunup every Sunday.

She came and stood inside the door. I happened to look up and see her there. She had entered so quietly that I hadn't heard her footsteps. I looked at her, and for a moment I did not know her.

Always slender, she was thin to the point of painfulness now. Her eyes were shadowed and the skin on her face seemed drawn and taut. Her hair was pulled back tightly and anchored close to her head. But the change was mostly around the mouth. She no longer looked young and untouched, with the soft mouth of a girl. Her lips were compressed and colorless like those of an old woman, a woman who has lived long and suffered much. A bitter woman. Two years had changed Hannah Jackson. They had indeed.

"I wanted to talk with you," she said. Her voice sounded harsh and rasping.

I motioned to a chair near my desk. "Sit down, Hannah," I said, sounding foolish and eager even to myself. "It's good to see you again."

She stared across at me, her eyes glazed and feverish. Why, she's ill, I thought, surprised.

Somehow she seemed to know what I was thinking. "I'm not sick," she said. "I know what I'm doing."

"Why did you come here, Hannah?" I asked as gently as I could. Because I knew that she owed us nothing, that we were the ones in debt to her.

"I came because I am ready to do it," she said, looking at me still in that strange feverish fashion. "I am ready to confess to the church that I have sinned in my love and in my marriage. I have to do it."

"Why?" I asked her. Because I couldn't understand it. Not when I was thinking that she and Terrell had made a strong world for themselves, a safe world, one that I envied in a way.

"Because I have to be forgiven," she said.

There was something frightening about her, about the way she sat there looking at me with those burning eyes. About the way she leaned forward and clutched my desk. Only this time I wasn't going to choose the least fearful way.

"There is only One to whom you must look for forgiveness. I feel sure that you have already been forgiven by Him." I spoke quietly, looking at her so that she could see that I was being as honest as I knew how.

"No," she said, the word falling heavy between us. "I want to go before the church."

"But why?" I couldn't understand it. "This church, it's nothing but a group of people, Hannah. Sinful people, like you are. Like I am. You don't have to ask our forgiveness. I knew that even when we asked it of you," I said, thankful for the chance to finally say it to her.

"No," she said. "I have to be forgiven. I want to do it. Today. This morning."

I sat there for a moment, trying to think what to do.

"Have you spoken to Terrell about this, Hannah?" I asked finally.

"No," she said quickly, for the first time taking her eyes from my face. She looked rapidly around the room, toward the window, toward the door. Then she raised her hand to her throat slowly. It was a familiar gesture with her, I suddenly remembered. Something I had seen her do many times. She looked back at me sadly. "I can't tell him," she said softly.

We sat there in silence, looking across the desk at each other. What was there to be said? Finally she rose and walked to the window. When she spoke again, her voice had resumed the harsh quality, the tearing, grating edge.

"He wouldn't understand, you know. Besides," she turned toward me, her body tense, her eyes blazing, "the sin is mine, Preacher. *Mine.* Do you hear? I'm the one being punished. I'm the one He is denying a child. Terrell—he has children. He has two sons. But I have nothing. Nothing, nothing, nothing!" She was almost shrieking the last. She came toward me, her hands outstretched, pleading.

"I have tried so hard, Preacher. I've prayed to Him constantly. Give me a baby. Please give me a baby. But He won't listen. I've promised Him that if He would give me a son, I would make that son into a minister. I promised Him that. Still He hasn't heard me. Because I'm not forgiven," she said, sobbing, and she knelt beside me, putting her head against the desk.

"Hannah, Hannah," I began soothingly, reaching out to her. Never in my life had I felt so helpless, so sad. "Hannah, let me take you home."

"No!" She jerked back from my hand. "I am going to confess to the church. Then God will forgive me. He will give me a baby then." She looked at me strangely, but with a wild determination. "He will forgive me then," she said. "I know He will."

"Will Terrell be able to forgive you, Hannah?" I asked.

She looked at me for a moment, then answered quietly. "He will have to."

SYE JOHN MORRISON

For two years I sat on my bench in front of Cabot's store and waited for Hannah Jackson to come riding down the middle of the town on that big, fancy horse. Yessir, I thought that one day she would come tearing through here hell-bent, showing all of us just how proud she was. It would have been a fine ending to it all. But that ain't the way it happened.

No sir, she just sat out there at Turkey Bend Ranch and ate her heart out. Oh, I finally did get to see somebody come racing through town on that horse, but the somebody was Secoria and this was a long time afterwards. A long time after Hannah had settled her account in a way nobody had foreseen. Not even Terrell.

It was quite a time from that night she was expelled at church until I set eyes on Hannah again. The next time I saw her was one Sunday morning. It must have been the Sunday she made her confession to the church.

I always get up early on Sundays, and I walk down to the bus station to pick up a newspaper and have a cup of coffee with Mattie Riggs. Mattie has to open early on account of the bus coming in from Austin at six-fifteen. It was in the spring, I think. A nice morning. I was walking slowly, looking round at everything, feeling pretty good. I like walking alone in the morning and looking over this town. It seems so quiet and still. I always feel like it belongs to me. And, in a way, it does.

Anyways, I was almost to the churchhouse when I saw her coming down the road. She had on old, faded clothes and she was covered with that kind of fine dust that gathers on the ranch roads. She was thin too, with her face sort of drawn. Matter of fact, it took me a good ten minutes before I knew who she was. It wasn't until she turned in at the church that I figured it out. She had been wearing a kerchief on her head. When she walked into the churchyard, the wind must have caught it and pulled it loose. It was only when I saw them yellow braids that I recognized Hannah.

Lord God, I said to myself. Lord God!

When I got to the bus station Mattie was sitting at the counter reading the funny papers.

"Give me that cup of coffee quick, Mattie," I said. "I done seen a ghost."

Mattie just kept on reading. "You're too old for that, Sye John," she said.

"No, Mattie," I answered. "I'm just old enough. Just old enough to know one when I see it." Mattie heaved herself off the bench and got me my coffee. She always has been a big woman, Mattie has.

"Well," she said, "another Sunday."

"Yes," I answered. "Another Sunday."

NELLIE BARTON

My brother Cyrus didn't like it at all when the church put Hannah Jackson out. All the way home from church he grumbled at me, telling me that we was wrong. But I held my tongue. When you're in the right, you don't have to defend yourself. And in the long run Hannah herself proved how right we were. It's like I told Myra Cabot. "Myra," I said, "if we hadn't stood firm like we did, Hannah would never have become the great Christian witness which she was." And of course Myra agreed with me.

I was sitting in church with Myra that Sunday when Hannah came back. We got out of Sunday school early and went into the sanctuary to sit until church time. It's cooler in there. Well, when we came in, we noticed this woman sitting in the back but we didn't pay her too much attention. I never thought at the time about it being Hannah. She was dressed so poorly, you know. And her clothes were all dusty. She had a scarf around her head. Not one of them silk kind, but the old-fashioned kind that's made of cotton cloth. Well, like I was saying, Myra and I sat down and were chatting when Myra looked around at that woman and gave a little gasp.

"What is it, Myra?" I asked, looking myself.

She turned back toward me quickly and said, "Don't look." She grabbed my arm.

"What ever are you getting so excited about?" I asked.

"That woman back there," she whispered.

"What about her?" I asked. "She looks like some cedar chopper to me."

"That's Hannah Jackson," Myra said, her face red with the surprise of it all.

"No!" I just couldn't believe it. But then I looked again. And it was. Even I could see that it was.

"What ever do you think she's doing here?" I said to Myra. But Myra only shook her head and pressed her lips together.

Well, by that time the church was filling up. You could see people looking at Hannah as they came in and before long they were turning around
in their seats and looking again. By the time the service started, everybody
knew who that woman in the back seat was. Nobody knew why she was
there, but it made for a lot of squirming during the sermon, I can tell you.

It just made you uncomfortable somehow. Seeing her there looking
so—well, so different. She used to have some pride in her appearance.
Myra leaned over and whispered to me, "She don't look like she's well."

All during the singing there was a great craning of necks and whisper-
ing in the congregation. Then Longstreet got up in the pulpit.

"I am not going to deliver the message that I had prepared for this
service," he said. Well! You can imagine the reaction to that. It was like
the whole room sort of took in their breaths. I just never did care much for
that man.

"Instead of the sermon," he continued, "there are two matters which
I would like for this church to consider. The first is something that I am
sure you all remember." He paused for a moment, then took a deep breath
and went on. "Two years ago this church withdrew its fellowship from one
Mrs. Hannah Troxler Jackson. It did so because the church felt she should
publicly confess and repent of a certain offense. At that time Mrs. Jackson
did not feel she could do this." Everybody was peeking around at her now.
She just sat there, watching the preacher with the strangest look in her eyes.

"I tell you she ain't well," Myra hissed in my ear.

"Mrs. Jackson came to me this morning," the preacher went on. "She
now feels that she can and must take this step. Is there any opposition to
the church hearing her at this time?" The preacher looked out over the
congregation. Of course nobody said anything. They were too surprised,
for one thing. Besides, nobody wanted to stand in her way.

"Since nobody seems opposed, Mrs. Jackson," Longstreet said, "you
may speak."

We all turned to watch her. She sat still for a moment, then slowly she
put her hands on the pew in front of her and pulled herself up. You should
have seen how thin that woman was! No wonder we didn't know her at
first! We all thought that she would speak from where she was, but no, she
stepped into the aisle and walked toward the front of the church.

Myra leaned over toward me. "She must have walked into town from
the ranch," Myra said. "Look at all that dust."

Well, she walked up to the front of the church and turned to face us. She stood there for a minute, her eyes darting around the building. She was as pale as a ghost. Finally her eyes seemed to fasten on something near the door. For a minute her mouth quivered, then she began to speak, so softly that I almost couldn't hear her.

"You asked me two years ago to say that I had sinned in my"—she hesitated for a second—"in my marriage. At that time I did not feel that I had." She kept looking at the back of the church, at just one spot, but she seemed to straighten up a little and her voice got a little stronger. "I did not feel it was a sin because I loved my husband. Now I know that I was wrong. It doesn't matter how much you love someone. That must not be allowed to come between you and God." She tore her eyes away from the door and looked around the church. "So I am confessing and repenting of my sin. I pray that you will forgive me and that God will forgive me." She stood for a moment, then turned toward the preacher. "That's all," she said, in a helpless sort of way.

The preacher leaned down toward her and said, "You may go now, Hannah." He spoke softly.

She started to walk up the aisle, only this time she continued past her pew and on to the door. Everybody turned around to watch her and what do you think we saw! There stood Terrell Jackson, right by the door. Right where he could hear all she had said.

"Heavens!" Myra said. "She must have been looking right at him."

Terrell held the door for her and they went out. Well, I don't need to tell you that the church was buzzing by this time. Preacher Longstreet had to almost shout to make himself heard.

"Is there anyone who objects to restoring Hannah Jackson to the full fellowship of this church?" he asked. But of course nobody objected. "Then she is once again a member in good standing," he said.

The buzzing began again, but the preacher hushed it by saying, "Please. There is one more matter to be put before you. I would like to announce my resignation as pastor of this church, effective two weeks from today." He paused for a moment and looked over the church row by row. Then he said quietly, "That is all. You are dismissed."

Well! You think we didn't have some goings-on that Sunday! I never saw anything like it before or since. Like a regular side show or something. It just beat all.

TERRELL L. JACKSON

I did not need Preacher Longstreet to send word to know where Hannah was. When I awoke and found her gone, I knew. I had seen her gradually deciding to do it; I had felt her slowly being pulled back to that church. Why didn't I stop her? Perhaps if I had said something to her, if I had told her exactly how I felt, she might not have done it. But I couldn't do it, because it had to be her decision. What kind of man would I have been if I had said to her, "Hannah, if you love me, you must not renounce me." Sounds foolish, doesn't it?

Besides, it wasn't that simple. She did love me, you see. I knew that. She loved me and she needed me. But there was something that she loved and needed more.

Oh, I had tried. God knows I tried. For two years I had turned and twisted and tortured myself trying to prove to her that we could have everything by simply having each other. And I had watched her grow thinner and quieter and more pale each day. I lied to myself about the reasons, of course. I kept telling myself that it was because we didn't have the baby; it was because she felt she was failing me by not giving me the son we both wanted. Yet all the time I knew that it would end back in that church. That didn't stop me from hoping, though. If it comes down to it, I said to myself, she won't be able to go through with it. She won't be able to say it.

Well, it was not the only time I've been wrong.

Toward the end of the two years I began to be desperate. I would cling to her and say, "Aren't I enough, Hannah? We don't need children to make our life complete. You are enough for me. Let me be enough for you." Then I awoke that morning and knew, even before I got out of bed, that she had gone back to the church, back to her God.

But, like I said, I still had hope. Even while I did my chores around the ranch, even after the Mexican boy came with the preacher's message, even

112

on the drive to the church, I kept hoping that she would come away with me without speaking.

I opened the door of the church and slipped inside just as the preacher began. I watched her walk to the front, and I thought that I could not stand the sight of her there, so very helpless, so very forlorn. For one wild moment I thought of going up there with her, whether to lead her away or simply to stand beside her I don't know. Then she saw me. She looked right at me while she spoke.

I have often wondered what that speech cost her. How much strength did it take for her to stand there and condemn us? For she knew as well as I that she was doing just that. She was condemning us to live our lives with a wall between us, a separateness that could not be overcome.

I remember that I felt rage; bitter, futile, impotent rage. At her, at myself, at life that had allowed me to hope and try and suffer and fail. But underneath the rage and overcoming it finally, I felt pity. It would have bothered you, Hannah, if you had known that I pitied you. And not only that day, but all your life.

We drove home without speaking. I stopped the truck in front of the house. "Go inside and clean up, Hannah," I said. "I'll be back for lunch." Then I went to check on some sheep that had been sheared the day before. Go about your business, I said to myself, it's all over now. No more fighting. You know where you stand.

There was some relief in that, the fact that I no longer had to dread it.

LETTER FROM GREGORY TREMAYNE
TO HIS FATHER, MOFFETT TREMAYNE,
WRITTEN NOVEMBER 6, 1960

Dear Dad,

I know you are going to wonder at me for writing you two letters in the same week and not asking for money in either one of them. I'm beginning to wonder at myself. The truth is, I am afraid that money won't help me. I don't know exactly what will, to be honest. I can't seem to buckle down to my work—or to anything else for that matter. Can't even seem to get interested in a girl. And you know that I've always been one with an eye for the girls ever since my first crush on Secoria Jackson.

Dad, I am afraid that I am not going to pass my courses unless I can make myself begin studying. Or at least make myself attend classes. Today I had every intention of going. Only when I was dressed I began walking and I walked right off the campus and through town to a cemetery on a hill outside the city limits. Then I went through the cemetery reading all the names and counting the angels on the tombstones. I didn't get back here until afternoon. I could understand myself better if it were spring, but it was cold and ugly today. One of those miserable, drizzling midwestern days.

Yes, I know that I am supposed to graduate from this fine old institution in the spring. Yes, I know that I will never be a lawyer and a credit to the family at this rate. Yes, I know that it is not like me to neglect my responsibilities. Or is it? What *is* like me? What am I like? Am I sure I want to be a lawyer? Am I sure what being a credit to my family means?

It sounds silly, I know, but it seems that my problem is not knowing what my problem is. Because I don't know what I myself am. That's what I need a course in, self-recognition. Only they don't have a professor here who can teach it.

Enough of this dribble. I suppose I'll close and write MY NAME IS GREGORY TREMAYNE five hundred times. That might help. But before I do, here is the real reason for my writing this letter: would you mind if I left school? Believe me, Dad, I am serious.

Please don't show this to Mother. I don't want her to worry.

As ever,
Greg

P.S. Have been wondering about Mrs. Jackson. Since she was kicked out of the church, how did she get back in? Ah, that ole time religion—

LETTER FROM MOFFETT TREMAYNE
TO HIS SON, GREGORY,
WRITTEN NOVEMBER 8, 1960

Dear Greg,

Hannah Jackson got back in the church by paying a price and a pretty big one. That is how you get anything in this world, but no doubt twenty-one years is sufficient time to learn that. You might say that Hannah chose between two things, only I doubt that she knew that she was choosing. We seldom do. And if we do know, we seldom have any indication as to which is the right choice. But enough of this. It is not what you wanted to hear.

In fact, I am not exactly sure what you did want to hear. And I am not sure what I should say to you or if I should say anything. I can't say that I see how leaving school would help you, but on the other hand, I don't want to be hasty about this. Do you have any idea where you might go if you left? Or does it matter?

I know that you will find this letter very unsatisfactory. I find it to be, myself. But you must understand that it is hard for parents to let their young undertake the perilous task of choice-making and price-paying. Because once on that path, there is no turning off of it.

Write me again when you have more concrete ideas as to what you would like to do. I may be able to help more then.

With love,
Dad

SYE JOHN MORRISON

So Hannah went back into the church. Ole Terrell, he fought hard, but he just couldn't quite keep her. That's the way it is, though. A man's best ain't always enough.

That was sure some Sunday what with Hannah repenting and the preacher resigning. I had been wondering what that preacher was waiting for. You could tell by watching him that he was waiting for something. I guess all along it was for her to give him some sign.

What happened down to that church was really none of my business. I had no truck with that church. But I heard about it, of course. And it kind of made me sick, the whole business did. I was sick of the people for pushing her into it and sick of her doing it and sick of Terrell's standing there watching. And I don't mean disgusted sick. No, it was a different sort of feeling. It was a kind of sad sickness. I guess I was sick of people and their goddamn searching for something that ain't ever been seen or felt or that even has a name. Something that's bigger than human and better. It was that kind of searching and hungering that brought the whole thing about.

Well, she got back in the church, and Terrell began working harder than ever on his ranch. Everything leveled off here in Fremond. We had a new preacher now, by the name of Carter. William Carter. And before another year had passed, Hannah and Terrell had a son. He was named Mark Thomas Jackson.

VIII

TERRELL L. JACKSON

Mark's birth seemed to mark a new beginning for us. He was a fine boy, strong and healthy. He was the son I had longed for, the son who would carry on my name and my ranch. He was our hope, not only for the future, but for the present. Through him Hannah and I were forever united in a shared love, a common pride.

Mark's birth meant much to me, but it transformed Hannah. She lay in her bed with the baby beside her wearing the radiance of a conqueror. She had been lovely as a young girl when I had first seen her. Then in those troublesome first years after our marriage she had seemed to fade, to grow old and tired. Now suddenly she burst forth again, only not in the same way as before. Then she had been a shy and lovely girl; now she was a beautiful and confident woman.

Confidence and assurance—that was what the baby seemed to bring to her. And with his birth the restraint that had grown between us seemed to melt away. She turned to me again, joyous and intriguing. No longer a frightened child, but an exciting woman. Yes, Mark's coming seemed to be the beginning for us in many ways.

We were very happy together those first years. When Mark was four, our daughter was born. She was named Secoria for my grandmother. Hannah had not been as well as she should have been, so I had sent her into town to stay when it drew near the time for the baby to be born. In case anything should happen suddenly, I wanted her to be near the doctor.

Mark stayed at the ranch with me. He was a sturdy, fearless child. All day he would follow me around the ranch without complaining or asking for help. The men were all partial to him and he loved being around them, being outdoors with the animals, around the barns and corrals. He was already driving Hannah crazy by running out of the house and down to the stables. She didn't like for him to be around the horses because she was afraid he would get hurt. But you couldn't keep him away.

I was watching him down at the stables one day, noticing his lack of fear, and I thought of the pony. It was a Shetland, not much bigger than a dog. I had seen it a couple of times when I had gone into Burnet to buy stock. So when Hannah went to stay in town, I decided that Mark and I would have a surprise for her when she came back home.

She didn't want to go, although the doctor had suggested that it would be best. "What will Mark do?" she asked me, frowning.

"Mark and I will make out," I answered. "We're big enough to care for ourselves."

"You won't watch after him," she protested. "You'll let him go down to the barns where anything could happen to him."

"I'll take care of him, honey," I said.

"You don't know how."

"I'll take care of him. I promise you."

Finally she gave in. But when I left her in her room at the hospital she clung to me and begged me again to watch over her baby. I became a little impatient.

"He's not a baby, Hannah," I said, taking her arms from around my neck. "And I'm capable of caring for my own son."

The next day Mark and I hitched a horse trailer to the pickup and drove to Burnet. When we came back home we had the pony. Mark called him Little Boy.

Little Boy was a gentle horse, accustomed to children and used to being ridden. The first day we had him I got Mark up early. As soon as he had his breakfast I dressed him and took him out to the stable. Manuel was waiting with Little Boy.

"What are we going to do, Daddy?" Mark asked me, clutching my hand.

"We're going to make a surprise for Mother," I said. I handed the boy over to Manuel.

"Teach him to ride that pony, Manuel. And you haven't got a lot of time. I want him able to stay on by the time the señora comes home."

Manuel nodded, his black eyes gleaming, his teeth shining in his dark face.

It was three and a half weeks before Hannah and the baby came home. That was enough time for Manuel to have the boy sitting his horse in a fairly decent way. As for Mark, he loved it. Manuel came to me one evening, pausing beside me but looking off into the distance as he talked.

"Mark," he said softly, "he is good on the horse. He is a strong boy."

I drove Hannah home in the morning. She was pale and weak but anxious to get to the ranch. "Take her on, Terrell," the doctor said, "or she's going to get sick from missing that boy so much."

Mark was waiting for us at the end of the lane.

"I got a surprise for you, Mother," he said, not even noticing the baby, not bothering to kiss his mother or return her embrace.

Hannah looked over at me, troubled. "I don't think he missed me," she said.

"Sure he did," I said. "He's just excited over the surprise."

But we waited until that afternoon to show her. When the sun was almost down I sent Mark down to the stable. "It's time," I said.

"You go on the porch, Mother, and wait," he said to Hannah.

Hannah and I sat together on the porch. It was cool now and the sky was beginning to be streaked with the colors of the sunset.

"Terrell," her voice was quiet, gentle, "are you disappointed about the baby? Are you sorry it's a girl?"

"Sorry?" I moved closer to her, puzzled, wondering what could have made her think I cared. "Why should I be?"

"Oh, I don't know," she said. "I just thought that perhaps you would have preferred another son."

"No." I smiled down at her and put my arm around her shoulders. "I'm perfectly happy with the son I have. In fact I'm glad the baby is a girl. We might as well divide it up," I said jokingly, "a boy for me, a girl for you."

She turned toward me then, her face seeming cold and strange in the pale light. "I don't know what you mean," she said in a flat voice.

Slowly I withdrew my arm from around her. "It was only a joke, Hannah," I said.

We heard Mark calling from around the house, "I'm coming, Mother. Get ready!" and they came into view, Little Boy walking placidly along, Manuel beside him, and Mark sitting confidently in the saddle. "Look, Mother, I'm a vaquero!" he shouted. Manuel smiled, reached out, and turned the horse toward us. They came on, the boy riding the pony, the shy Mexican smiling down at the ground as he walked beside them. They were a lovely sight against the yellow and red sky, against the brown and yellow land.

Beside me Hannah stood up and walked to the porch railing. "Manuel!" she called, her voice harsh and tight. "Get him down from there!" Then she was facing me, her face rigid and stern. "I won't have it! Do you hear me, Terrell? I won't have it!" Then she went into the house.

"Daddy?" whimpered the boy from his horse. "Didn't she like me? Didn't she like the surprise?"

"She's tired, son. That's all," I finally managed to say. "Get him down, Manuel."

"*Sí.*" He turned toward Mark.

"No, Daddy. Let me ride him back. I have to help Manuel take the saddle off."

"All right," I answered automatically. "Just take him away."

When I walked inside she was standing looking down at the sleeping baby. Her back was straight and her face had the same hard set to it, as though it had been cast in stone.

"Why did you do it, Hannah?" I asked. Because I didn't understand it. Because the boy was young and proud and if she loved him she should have at least acknowledged those very facts.

She whirled on me. "You're not going to do it, Terrell. You're not going to raise him to be a rancher. I can't let you."

"Hannah, what do you mean? What are you talking about?" I walked toward her to touch her, to try to understand this crazy meaningless talk. But she moved out of my reach.

"Terrell, he can't be a rancher. He just can't be. And you mustn't let him grow up to want it."

"But I *want* him to want it," I said. "You've always known that."

She came to me then and put her hands on my shoulders. "He has no choice," she said. "He's promised. Before he was even born I promised him to God," she said.

And there it was.

"You can't have him, Terrell," she said. "I promised him to God." It was that simple to her. All she had to do was to say it; that was all. By the simple forming of the words her—and mine too—*our* son's life was wrapped up neatly, tied in a bow, put away.

"You must be out of your mind, Hannah," I said.

"No," she answered, "not now. *Then* I was a little, maybe, but not now." She looked at me suddenly, her face fierce and twisted. "You don't know what those days were like. You can never know. It was like living in a vacuum. Like being in a completely empty space. I felt as though I were deaf, dumb, blind. I tell you, you can never know! It wasn't like that for you, Terrell. You had your ranch. Besides, He never mattered to you, God didn't. I kept saying that He didn't matter to me, that I didn't care. But I was lying to myself and I knew it. All of a sudden it was like I was a child again. I felt the same way as when my mother left me. Deserted. Alone. Completely alone. When I was a child I would run to the springs and look for my mother, call to her, but there was no answer. Now God had gone away from me too. I knew He had. I could feel the emptiness around me."

She paused for a moment, then rushed on. "When He would not give us children, it was because of me. Because He had to break my pride and my will. And He did. He made me do the thing I had said I would never do. He made me crawl back to the church. And He also took my promise that I would make Mark into a man of God, that I would return my child to His service."

I looked across the room at her, loving her foolishness, her childish faith. No matter how far from her I went she always drew me back to her by letting me see, behind the infinite sadness of her eyes, that lost and haunted child who lay hidden, demanding, selfish, at the bottom of all that she was and thought and did.

I tried to explain it to her. "It's not like that, Hannah. Nothing is that simple."

"That is why I'm so sorry about the baby," she continued as though I had never spoken. "I so wanted to give you a boy to make up for this one that I can't let you have." She walked over to the sleeping baby and looked down at it. "But it's only a girl," she said.

"Hannah, listen to me," I said, going to her, speaking to her as though she were a child. "You mustn't talk this way. You were guilty of nothing but love. You did nothing wrong. You do not owe God—or anybody else—anything. And as for Mark, you can't make him into anything that he doesn't want to be. Neither can I. He is our son and we'll love him and have plans for him, surely. All parents do. But in the end he will be what he wants to be, what he has to be, regardless of us. A man only belongs to himself, Hannah."

"Not Mark," she said, taking her hands from mine. "Mark belongs to God. I *have* to see to that, Terrell. And I will."

But I wouldn't let her get away from me. I pulled her into my arms and rocked her there, stroking her hair, talking to her. She seemed like a foolish, stubborn child. How immeasurably sad that is. To hold a woman in your arms and know that she is ruled by a lost and frightened child.

At least that is how it seemed to me then. She seemed a child saying, I can't break my promise for I crossed my heart.

But how can I feel about it now? For she kept her promise.

SYE JOHN MORRISON

Hannah and Terrell Jackson had three children. And three more different people you are never going to see under one roof than them kids.

By all rights the Jacksons shouldn't have had any but the first one. In many ways he was the only one they did have. For by the time the other two came along and got old enough for noticing, Hannah and Terrell were so tied up in fighting over the first one that the others were left to fend for themselves.

Not that Mark wasn't worth fighting over. He was just what a person would want in a boy, I guess. Nice-looking kid, strong, healthy, bright. Polite and well mannered. The kind of a boy a man can be proud of. Terrell was, too. About as proud as ever I've seen. He kept the boy with him as much as he could. "Yessir," he used to say, clapping the boy on the shoulder, "Mark's going to be my partner one of these days."

Well, that was something for the boy to look forward to. For Terrell had made Turkey Bend into a fine and prosperous ranch. The other men would shake their heads. "Terrell's got his pa's gambling luck," they would say. Whatever it was— luck, devotion, hard work—it was paying off. By the time the boy was ten years old Terrell was not only back where he started when Hannah came into his life, but he was even ahead of that. When a boy could look forward to a partnership in something like Turkey Bend Ranch it was no mean outlook.

But Terrell couldn't keep the boy with him as much as he would have liked because Hannah was doing her part. She had her claws in too, and she wasn't letting go. "I depend on Mark," she used to say. "He's the one who always cares for Mother."

So they went at it, each tugging and pulling at the boy. He's going to be a rancher, Terrell would say, tugging his way. He's going to be a preacher, Hannah would say, tugging her way. And the boy?

Well, he was a strong boy. But all the pulling at him was bound to tell.

Even as a little kid he was the serious type. I used to get him to sit down with me and I'd try to kid him, to josh him around like I did the other kids. But he would only watch me with those bright, serious eyes—they was dark eyes, like Hannah's—and he would never seem to laugh or even understand what there was to laugh about. Oh, he was always polite. I guess that's what I remember most about him. How very hard he tried to please.

As for the other two, now that's a different story. It was a shame that Terrell and Hannah was too tied up in their fight over Mark. For they had sitting before them two other chances—and good ones too—to find what they wanted. Terrell had his rancher, a natural-born one. Only she happened to be a girl. And Hannah had her preacher, maybe. Only he was a quiet shy boy whose health was never too good.

Now kids are a lot like animals. They ain't too smart but they can sense things. It didn't take Secoria and Tim long to sense that they were more or less on the outside. So they naturally found their own ways to get their share of the attention. Tim was sick a lot; Secoria became the daredevil.

I never got to know Mark too well, but the other two, I spent time with them. Yessir, we was friends from the first day that they came up to my bench.

It must have been when the girl was about six. Tim was a little feller, but she had him in tow, pulling him along as fast as his legs would go. She always looked after Tim, Secoria did. She pulled him right up to the bench and stopped in front of me. She had a mass of dark red hair even then and it was tumbled all over her head. She had dark eyes too. Only they weren't serious and sad but blazing and fierce.

"How come you've got a stick for a leg?" she asked in that voice that was already deep and hoarse.

"I got my other leg cut off in an accident," I said.

"Oh," she said. "Did a horse fall on it?"

"No. It was a lumbering accident. I got it pinned under some logs when I was loading a truck."

"Oh. I thought maybe you were a vaquero."

"Just a lumberjack," I said, tickled at her disappointment. She only liked stories with horses in them.

She was quiet for a moment, looking at the peg. Then she said, "Did it take you long to learn to walk on this stick?"

"It's a peg," I said. "It took a while."

She looked up at me. "Can I touch it? The peg?"

I nodded and she put her hand out and softly stroked the peg. "I think it's nice," she said. "Touch it, Tim," she said, tugging at the boy's hand. But he hung back, his eyes wary and a little frightened. He wasn't looking at the peg but at me.

"It's okay, son," I said softly. "It doesn't hurt." My heart went out to the little feller standing there. He was a skinny little guy, not much to look at. But right from the first I liked him. Maybe it was because I had waited over thirty years to see Mora Troxler's eyes again. And here they were repeated in her grandson. They were a deep shade of blue, almost violet. And like Mora's, they were smudged and shadowed, so deep and lovely that only a face of great beauty could contain them successfully. This little boy, with his thin narrow face, his long nose, his pale delicate skin, didn't have the looks to balance them.

"It's all right, son," I said again, but he had already started to cry, pulling out of Secoria's grasp and turning away from us. She stooped quickly and gathered him up. She was small, and he made an armful for her. She staggered a bit and I reached to help her, but she recovered by herself.

"It's okay," she said. "I carry him a lot. He gets scared easy," she explained.

They started away. When they had gone a few steps down the street, she put him down and wiped his face with her skirt. She talked to him in a low voice, soothing and gentle. Finally she turned back to me. "We'll come to see you again," she said. Then away they went with her pulling him along with her.

SECORIA JACKSON

I have loved four people in my lifetime. That's some sort of accomplishment, I guess. To manage to care about four other human beings. Of course three of those I loved in my childhood when loving was still relatively easy. And of the three, only one lived to realize it. When he did understand how I loved him, it was too late.

Yes, I think Terrell knew that I had loved him. But Manuel and Timothy, I'm not sure about them. Because I was too young to know how to tell them. Too young to even know that I did, I suppose.

Manuel was my comforting love. By the time I was three, I was following him about the yard. By the time I was five, we spoke Spanish together. He was the gentlest man I have ever known. And in many ways the strongest. Through all the wild, untamed, rebellious days of my childhood, it was only Manuel who could control me, who could make me obey.

Yes, I was a difficult child and I gloried in it. Just as I have gloried in my difficult youth and now my difficult womanhood. No doubt I shall one day be a difficult spinster. But when I was a difficult child, perhaps it was because I wanted some gentle voice to control me, who knows? Perhaps that is all I have ever wanted.

Manuel was that voice, that control. And he was the one person who didn't seem to prefer Mark to me. Probably because I was better with the horses. Mark was competent with them, yes, but I was gifted. So I became Manuel's favorite. It didn't take me long to discover that I could replace Mark in Manuel's eyes. So I made a point of it. Because Mark and I were deadly enemies from as early as I remember.

Poor Mark. He never knew how much I hated him. Or if he did, he never knew why. And it wasn't really his fault. It was theirs—Hannah's and Terrell's. Or maybe just Terrell's. Because I think that Hannah and I had settled our relationship while I was still in the cradle. I had known from the first that there was no hope that she would ever care for me. But Terrell—I

127

still thought that he might some day love me. There were times when he would take me on his lap and play with my hair, calling me Miss Fuzzy top and Chief Red-on-the-Head. I could make him laugh too, with my wild romping and feats of physical daring. Yes, I could make him tease me and laugh at me and scold me. But I could not make him proud; I could not make him care. Only Mark could do that.

So I hated Mark. And I decided that I would be better at everything than he was. I was four years younger, I was a girl, but I would show Terrell that I was his true son. Only it never quite worked. Yes, I could ride and handle horses better. Yes, I learned as much or more about the ranch. Yes, I could eventually stay as long, work as hard, and understand it all better. But it was too late. For by the time Terrell realized that he could make a rancher out of me, it no longer mattered to him. The drought had come; Mark had gone. By the time I could offer the gift that I had always thought he wanted, his desire for it was gone.

My third love—and the most bitter in many ways—was Timmy. I think that I loved Timmy simply because somebody had to and it seemed that I was the only one to do it. He and Hannah were never cold to each other like she and I were. No, she fussed over him, was concerned about him; yet she never loved him. It was more as though she were trying to make him strong enough to stand by himself so that she wouldn't have to be involved with him. Or perhaps she was simply trying to make him into the kind of boy that Terrell would like so that she could have Mark by herself. And Terrell always called Tim a mommy's boy as though he wanted Tim to belong to Hannah. Nobody really wanted Tim. Not even Secoria. I only took him because he had to have somebody. And eventually I deserted him too.

He was a funny little gnome, with his narrow face and his big bruised-looking eyes. His arms and legs were long and scrawny. He was clumsy and delicate and easily frightened. But he was also sensitive and kind and loving. With Manuel and Terrell and even with that fourth and grown-up love I consider myself even, finished. It is only to Timmy that I still cry out in the night, that I still beg for forgiveness. I loved Timmy but not enough. And not in time to help him.

TIMOTHY LOGAN JACKSON

I dwelt in the world as one moves through a dream, suspended and alone. Looking always for a mother, a sister, a father, a brother, and on every hand seeing nothing save faces twisted and tortured until torture and life became one for me. Until my flesh could no longer bear the pain of my breathing.

Secoria was a shadow to protect me from the sun. When the shadow left me, the light was scorching and blinding. And the fear, which had always been the air I breathed, became one with the light shining upon me until I could not find rest upon the earth.

I came into life afraid. Like any man. Only I embraced my fear, I loved my fear, I became my fear. Until finally I was gone and only the fear remained.

It was a brief life. I was a stranger who loved the dark and feared the light.

MOFFETT TREMAYNE

I was in my first year at Texas University when the twin disasters of the Great Depression and the Big Drought advanced upon Fremond and slowly began squeezing the life from the town. It was late spring when the bank failed. The town was already reeling from a dry fall and winter and the eagerly awaited spring had not only failed to bring moisture but brought instead this new worry. Woe be unto man when both nature and money fail him.

When the bank closed my dad had to call me home from school. He met me at the train station and we walked slowly through the town together. The dust lay over all the streets, over the trees, seemed to lie heavy and unmoving on the air.

"There's going to be another duster," Dad said.

"Seems like it." I hated the dust storms with their choking air, their eye-stinging, nose-burning darkness swirling inescapably around you.

"It's a hard time for everybody," he said. "The ranchers' land blowing away. The bank gone. Your having to leave school. It's hard for everybody."

"Yes," I answered in the seriousness of adolescence, "it's not an easy time."

He looked over at me slyly, amused. "But then, no time is easy when you're nineteen," he said. "Take it from me." He put his arm around my shoulders and smiled at me. "Your mother is going to cry when she sees you, son. She's already made up her mind."

We were walking along like that, smiling together, when we met Terrell Jackson. He was coming toward us on the sidewalk. When he saw Dad, he stopped.

"Thought you were leaving here, Tremayne," he growled, his eyes bloodshot. He was dressed in dusty work clothes and he had not shaved in several days. His beard was beginning to gray and so was his hair. I

130

could smell the whiskey on his breath, but his manner was deliberate and controlled.

"Leaving next week, Terrell," Dad said. "Got me a job up in Dallas."

"You've always been a smart man," Terrell said gruffly. "Leave before the damn place blows away. That's what I should do. Leave this goddamn dustbowl." Then he walked away as steady as could be. A trifle too steady.

Dad and I went on toward the house. "Terrell has a new boy, born a couple of days ago," Dad said. "Named him Timothy Logan. The Logan is for Terrell's father."

"I guess he was celebrating," I said.

"Terrell celebrates that way quite a bit these days."

"A serious thing, then?" I asked.

"Not yet," said Father. "Not yet."

We turned in at the house and Dad stopped in the yard. "I'm sorry, Moffett," he said. "I wanted to help you be a lawyer."

"It's okay, Dad," I answered. "I can make it on my own."

And I did. I worked on construction, picking fruit, whatever I could find. Eventually I became a lawyer and returned to Fremond. By the time I made it back home, Terrell Jackson's celebrations had become his way of life.

NELLIE BARTON

I always judge the strength of a Christian by the burdens they have to bear. Take Hannah Jackson. That poor woman had more than her share, I can tell you.

First, there was her husband. Now men are enough trouble any time, but when you get one like Terrell Jackson, well, it's a wonder to me that any woman can keep her faith when she's yoked to a man like that. Not only was he not a Christian, not only did he scorn the church, but he drank. And that's a curse no woman ought to have to bear. There is nothing that can try a woman's faith like being tied to a weak, drunken man.

Then there was that girl of hers. A wilder creature never hit this countryside. Most of the stories about her don't bear repeating, and there didn't seem to be one thing Hannah could do with her. Her behavior was a disgrace almost from the time she was a little thing.

And finally, there was that last boy of hers, Timothy. Poor thing was sickly from the time he drew his first breath. Then he did that terrible thing. I once knew a preacher who said that taking your own life was the unforgivable sin, for it was imposing your own will instead of allowing God's will to govern you. Which makes perfect sense to me. I guess it was the weakness that drove Terrell to drink that Timothy inherited.

But no matter how much pain and hardship God tried Hannah with she just seemed to grow stronger. The more that happened to break her spirit, the firmer she seemed to grow. I used to tell Myra Cabot that it was an inspiration to me to see that woman walking with her head high. She knew how to keep her dignity and her faith, Hannah did.

Of course she did have Mark. At least he proved to be a credit to his mother. It's like I told Myra, if a good Christian woman perseveres in her faith, then God's not going to let her go empty-handed. And I believe that. I sure do. Hannah Jackson was as good an example of that as I have ever seen.

IX

ENTRY IN THE DIARY OF
MARK THOMAS JACKSON,
MARCH 11, 1938

Today I am fourteen years old. That is a pretty important age. Mother says that in the next few years I shall be making decisions that will influence my whole life, so the next ten years are going to be my most important ones. In those years I shall decide what I'm going to be, how I'm going to spend the rest of my life. It makes me feel a little scared, but excited too.

We're going to have a family party tonight. Mom wanted me to have some friends over, but I didn't want to. I didn't feel like that kind of a party. Maybe a guy shouldn't feel serious on his birthday, but I do. I feel serious a lot these days.

I bet I know what Secoria will give me—another blasted diary. It's just as well. I've nearly used this one up.

SECORIA JACKSON

There is one advantage in growing older. You can begin to divide your life into a neat, easily discernible pattern. From here to here, you can say, I was a child. This particular event marked the beginning of my adolescence. Here I became an adult. The design becomes plain, the whole whirling chaos of experience takes on an order: a beginning, a middle, an end.

I can remember clearly the day my childhood ended. It was on Mark's fourteenth birthday. We were planning to have a family celebration in the afternoon, so early in the day Father took Tim and me into town to buy presents for Mark. I bought the same thing I had given Mark since I was five years old—a diary. Timmy took a long time deciding on a gift. Finally he bought a pocketknife. It was small and delicate with two shining blades and a smooth black handle.

Tim and I wrapped the packages when we got home. Then we carried them downstairs and put them on the table with the birthday cake. They were the only two presents there.

"I wonder where Mother and Dad's presents are," Timmy said.

"They're probably too big for the table," I answered, not without a trace of jealousy.

We saved the opening of the presents until after dinner, but when we all gathered around the table there were still only two presents. There were, however, two envelopes: one a heavy manila folder; the other a business envelope, white, with Mark's name typed across it. Mark reached across and took Timmy's present first.

"I already know what Secoria's present is," he said, grinning. He took the knife out of the tissue paper gently. "Gee, Tim," he said, "it's swell. It really is." He was a little surprised—and pleased. I looked at Tim who was blushing and thought of how much time he had taken to find the right gift. Suddenly I was ashamed of my selfishness, my jealousy, my foolish disregard of everybody but myself.

"Don't bother about mine, Mark. It's the same ole thing," I said, for he was taking my package now.

"I want to see what color it is this year," he teased. It was a nice color, a deep blue with gold lettering. It had a lock too with two small gold keys. "It's nice, Secoria," Mark said seriously, "and I did need a new one. My old one is filled up." But his kindness, the nice way he handled it, only made me feel worse.

"Well," said Terrell, trying to be jovial and joking but betraying his excitement, "that's the end of the birthday presents. All you have left are a couple of letters." That was all Dad had to say to plunge me back into my jealousy.

"Maybe this one has money in it," Mark said, opening the white envelope. "It's about the right size." But he only took out a piece of white paper with typed instructions.

"Go to the loading pen and look inside. Everything you find in there belongs to you," Mark read aloud. He looked up at Terrell puzzled, thinking about the pen, remembering the sheep that had been sorted and put in it during the day.

"Dad," he said, "the sheep you put in there today, you mean they are mine? You're giving me my own sheep?" His voice had risen with his excitement, his comprehension. He got up and walked over to Dad. "You mean they belong to me?"

"They're yours, Mark. You are a real rancher now," Terrell said quietly, reaching into his pocket. "Here's an account book for you. You're in business for yourself."

Mark reached out and took the book. "Gee, Dad, I don't know what to say," he began, tears in his eyes.

"No need to say anything," Terrell answered. "Just make money off those sheep."

Mark turned to Hannah. "What do you think about that, Mother? I've got my own sheep now."

But Hannah only said, "I think you have one more present to open."

"I almost forgot," Mark said, grinning. "Excited, I guess. I hadn't expected to have my own sheep for a while yet." He reached for the brown envelope. Out of it came a large booklet with a picture of an ivy-covered brick building. Lettered in gold across the top were the words "St. Mark's School for Boys." There was a letter too.

"It's addressed to Mother," Mark said. "'Dear Mrs. Jackson: We are very pleased to inform you that your son, Mark Thomas, has been accepted as a student in our school for the term beginning September 15, 1938. We are looking forward to visiting with you and your family in June. If you should have any questions before then, do not hesitate to write us.'" Mark's voice trailed off and he dropped the letter into his lap. "St. Mark's," he said strangely, looking at Mother.

"What the hell—" exploded Terrell, but Hannah was one jump ahead of him.

"I thought you might like to go off to boarding school, Mark," she said. "Some place where you could get a decent education, where you could study Latin and Greek."

"Latin and Greek be damned," said Terrell. "Just what the hell game are you playing, Hannah? You're not sending my boy off to any damn church school. Not while there's breath in my body."

She turned her gaze on him, level and serene. She did not even raise her voice. "He's going to have the best, Terrell. He's not going to be wasted out here on this ranch."

Mark was looking from one to the other with frightened eyes, trying desperately to find a way to pacify them, to please them. Timmy moved close to me. We stood together a little outside the three of them, watching.

"Secoria," Timmy half whispered, half whimpered.

"Shhh," I hushed him, wanting to see it happen, wanting them to fight and argue, to pull Mark first one way, then the other. For somehow I knew that this was the last one, the one that would decide the winner. And who knows? Maybe Tim and I could share the loser. "Be quiet," I said to Tim, putting my arm around him.

"I refuse to pay a penny for him to go away to school," Terrell said, his face drawn and white with anger. He was standing over Hannah threateningly while she just sat calmly looking up at him.

"You don't have to," she answered quietly. "I have the money from Aunt Minnie," she said. "It will be enough."

"Mother," Mark said, "I know you were thinking about how much better it would be for me. I mean, I know it's a good school and all that. But I have my sheep. I can't leave right now. Maybe next year I could—"

But Terrell rushed in. "He doesn't want to go, Hannah. And I'll be damned if you'll make him."

Mother looked at Mark then, for one long moment, a look so cold, so unrelenting, that I knew he could not stand against it. "Very well," she said, getting up and leaving the room. She walked to the door and went out, never looking back and closing the door behind her softly.

"Dad," Mark said hesitantly, "maybe I should take a while to think it over. I might like the idea after I thought about it. It was just, well, it was so new to me—"

But Terrell was blinded by his own anger and selfishness. "No," he shouted, furious, "you're not going! You hear me, you're not going!"

"But, Dad," Mark said, pleading, his handsome face twisted with his efforts at holding back the tears. He had tried so hard to keep everything in balance, to make them both happy.

But Terrell's voice had a hard and cutting edge to it now, a meanness, a mocking tone. "I said no. What are you, anyway," he asked, "some sissy mother's boy?"

Mark drew back as though he had been struck. His face went pale, frozen. For the first time I noticed how much he looked like Hannah.

"No," he said. "I'm not anybody's boy." And he got up from his chair then. With dignity. Yes, I know he was only fourteen, only a child. And I was a child too. But I tell you he got up with dignity and gathered his presents together and went quietly up to his room. We were left alone, Tim and Terrell and I.

Terrell stood for a moment in the center of the room, then he went to the sideboard and took out a bottle. He started to pour a drink, but instead he grabbed the bottle and rushed out the door.

"Manuel," he hollered as he went across the yard to the truck. "Manuel." A few minutes later the truck roared out of the drive with Daddy driving and Manuel sitting beside him.

I turned to Timmy. "You want to go down to the pen and see the sheep?" I asked him. "Maybe Dad will give them to us now."

"He can't," said Tim. "They belong to Mark."

"Mark won't need them," I answered, sure of myself. "He's going away to school."

I was no longer a child. I had seen the battle; I had wanted it. And I had understood it. So I was part of it, guilty like the others.

I looked over at Tim. He was standing by the sofa with tears in his eyes. "Come on, crybaby," I said roughly, "you're going to see some sheep."

I grabbed his hand and pulled him from the room and out of the house.

"I don't want to, Secoria," he said.

"You're going to," I answered, jerking his arm cruelly. I couldn't bear his innocence.

SYE JOHN MORRISON

There ain't nothing so hard for a man to find as a place for his anger. A man grown up and settled with a life planned and ordered, he ain't got the time nor the privacy for shaking his fist at the sky. And when enough outrage gets stored up inside a man, something is going to give way sooner or later.

Of course, with Terrell Jackson, it wasn't all anger. It was lots of things: bewilderment, frustration, disappointment. But at the base of all those other things—and coloring them—was rage, pure and simple.

The Depression hit Fremond harder than some places because here it came coupled with a three-year drought. It gave us some hard years, a decade of them. And when it was over, the town that came out of that bad time was changed. Some of the names that had been big here from the founding day were gone, swallowed up. Ranches changed hands three, four times that had been in the same family since Texas belonged to the Mexicans. Some of the places now belonged to absentee owners, the first we ever had round here. Men from Dallas, San Antone—some corporations even—they bought up the land. In some instances the old owners stayed on as foremen, but more often they packed their bags and left for good. The young people had gone too, most of them never to return. The state had built a new highway. This new road didn't bother to come through town but passed by a mile away. Yeah, the view from the bench in front of Cabot's General Store had changed. More and more I seemed to be watching the past while the future rolled down that glistening new pavement a mile away. I said as much to Moffett Tremayne when he came back to Fremond in '39. But he just said that I was getting old and the past was easier for the old to see.

Be that as it may, I had plenty to content myself with. I could sit and watch Terrell Jackson trying to find something to do with all his fury. By the time the bad years came, Terrell was already fighting with all his might on two fronts. There was his battle with Hannah. He didn't seem to be

139

doing so good there. Every time I would see her, she looked stronger and more sure of herself. And every time I saw Terrell, he looked more baffled and worn. If love is a battle for possession—and there are some of us who think that's what it's all about—then it was easy enough to see who was winning.

His other battle, the one for the boy, was still open. He was, in fact, even a little ahead. For the boy was young and active, more a creature of the body than of the mind and spirit. He liked the life of the ranch. But of course this was a harder war to tally. Because, like I said before, the boy wasn't easy to read. He wanted to please them both, you could see that. Now what was going to happen when he decided to please himself was still an open question.

All these worries had begun to take their toll even before the drought years came to add new fuel to the flames. Terrell had already been looking around for a way to "vent his rage," so to speak, and I wasn't surprised when he found it. It was a solution as old as man.

Not that the drinking was a problem in those days. It was an occasional thing, scarcely noticed save by them what had nothing more to do than watch others. But it was there and ready, just waiting for the anger to grow so big that there was no help for it. Then the drinking would step in and supplant it.

Well, the depression came and with it the drought. Terrell had a new war on his hands: the struggle to hang on to his land. And hang on he did where a lot of men who had nothing else to fight for let go. But this battle took its toll too. The drinking became heavier and heavier, although still under control.

By '38 he was pretty much in the clear on the ranch. Things were looking up; he was making money again. A breathing space, you might say. Then out of nowhere came the last straw. At least it came out of nowhere for me. I wasn't expecting things to happen as they did nor so fast.

It was about three o'clock in the morning when I awoke to the sound of sirens on the new highway. Some fool done smashed himself up in his automobile, I said and turned over to go back to sleep. It wasn't long, though, before the phone in the hall began to ring. I live in a boarding house, you see. Well, that damn phone rang for five minutes or longer before Mrs. Malone, the landlady, answered it. Then I heard her go down the hall and knock on the door of the doctor who lived in the last room. "Dr. Brennan," she says, "the hospital wants you over there right away." By this time I was awake real good, so I went to the door and called to her.

"What is it, Mrs. Malone?"

"It's Terrell Jackson," she said, her mouth drawn down tight in an attempt to hide the fact that she wasn't wearing her dentures. "He's done run himself into a carload of Mexicans and nearly killed 'em all. You might know he was drunk." And she went off down the hall, muttering disapprovingly under her breath. Which she does any time of the night or day, dentures or no dentures.

I was leaving the house the next morning when I met the doctor coming home. His face was drawn and tired and he needed a shave.

"Well, Doc, it must have been a bad one," I said.

He stopped and lit a cigarette, his hand shaking ever so slightly. "Could have been worse, I guess," he said. "Killed three. Two hurt. One walked away."

"What about Terrell Jackson?" I asked.

"He's the sonofabitch that walked away," he answered.

By the time I got down to Cabot's store everybody was talking about the wreck. About how Terrell came roaring down the old road to where it intersected the new highway and how he didn't even stop or look but took out onto the new road and about how he hit the Mexicans broadside and then they both went in the ditch and his truck turned over. Manuel was pinned beneath the wreckage. The Mexicans lost one old man, the grandfather, and one child, a small boy. The father had a broken arm, the mother some cuts and bruises. Terrell didn't even get a cut.

"God takes care of drunks," John Cabot said.

Two days later they buried Manuel in the ranch graveyard after the funeral down at the Catholic chapel where all the Mexicans worshiped. The day of the funeral Hannah came into town and bought a wardrobe trunk to pack Mark's clothes in. "He's going away to school," she told John Cabot. "St. Mark's," she said.

"I think that's real wise, Hannah, I surely do," John said, giving her one of his significant, holy looks. John Cabot was just born narrow and ignorant I guess.

TERRELL L. JACKSON

It all starts with one tiny crack in the foundation and no matter how a man tries to repair and bolster and cover over, the crack will grow. One day there will be the last ounce added and the strain becomes too much. All that's left is shattered fragments, jagged edges of memory, a ruin.

That is how it happened with me. The crack appeared the first time I was afraid. Afraid of losing Hannah, afraid that all I had dreamed and dared was in vain. Then that very fear of losing was what made the loss inevitable.

I sat in the corridor of the hospital and waited for the doctor to come out and tell me that Manuel was dead. I had known from the moment I saw him lifted into the ambulance that he could not live, but I had to hear the words. While I waited I realized that the fear was gone. I could not be afraid any longer, for all that I had feared had come to pass. Inside me I felt all the empty space, all that reaching, stretching, twisting nothingness where for years the fear had been pushing and shoving, straining to get out, driving me deeper into fury and despair and loneliness. Now there was nothing. Only years to be spent rummaging inside the empty shell of self that had been burned away by my own dread.

The doctor came out. His words were quick and to the point. Manuel and the others were dead. The doctor had known me for a long time, and he had no pity. Nor did I require any.

"You have destroyed three lives, Terrell," he said, looking at me with his cool gray eyes that had flecks of yellow in the pupil. I looked at those eyes and thought that he had made a conservative estimate of the damage.

I walked out of the hospital to begin the long waiting, the years of wandering through the broken pieces of my loves, my passions, my hopes, my errors. Years of watching the seed of my fear bear fruit. Years of biding my time in the world, reminiscing.

A man who lives with fear, is driven by it, feels its cold pressure on his chest with every breath, he is lost when at last the fear is gone. For it leaves him nothing, not even self-respect.

Hannah and I slept apart from that night. We lived together in a suspended world where we shared the routine divisions of days into hours and hours into minutes. She tolerated my weakness; I tolerated hers. She pitied my drinking; I pitied her pride. But we no longer hurt each other. For when one adversary is dead, there can no longer be conflict, can there?

SECORIA JACKSON

They buried Manuel on a cold gray March day with the wind roaring out of the west and cutting through the clothes of the mourners with icy, knifing thrusts. Everything was gray—sky, land, trees, even the coffin which I had selected with Hannah's help. We had gone to the funeral home, Hannah and I, soon after Terrell arrived home and told us that Manuel was dead. Hannah had awakened me, her face pale and ghostly in the early dawn light.

"Wake up, Secoria," she said. "Get dressed and come downstairs." She spoke softly, but something in her voice—some curious note, some fine-honed edge—roused me instantly from sleep and warned me. Warned me that, in its slow circling through the night, my world had shuddered, been shaken somehow, and a part of it had crumbled away. I pulled my jeans on quickly in the cold half-light and walked down the steps in my stocking feet carrying my boots. The kitchen was warm, bright with light, fragrant with the smell of breakfast. Terrell was seated at the table. I shall never forget his face. It was a mask the color of ashes, with his eyes staring out cold and dead and lifeless, yet somehow burning, burning. With pain. Nothing about him but those horrid, red-rimmed, painful eyes seemed alive. The rest of his face sagged and folded and bent into lines of decay and defeat.

I ran to him and put my arms around him, laid my cheek against his. "What happened, Daddy? What has happened?" I asked.

Very slowly he took my arms away from his shoulders and gently pulled me onto his lap, staring at me out of those terrible lost eyes. "Manuel is dead, Secoria," he said, his voice hollow, empty. "I wrecked the truck. I killed Manuel."

I pushed away from him, repulsed by his face, by those cruel merciless words. Hating him. Filled with hatred for him because I knew instantly it was true.

"No," I screamed at him. "No, no, no! You didn't kill him. It was an accident." I was sobbing blindly. "Please. No. No, no, no."

Hannah came to me and put her arms around me. For once I yielded to her embrace and lay sobbing on her shoulder. "Go upstairs and put on a dress," she said gently. "We must go into town and care for Manuel."

The coffin was austere, made of a gray metal. They laid Manuel's poor broken body against the gray watered silk lining and carried him to the little Catholic chapel where the priest said Mass, the Latin rolling, surging, intertwining like music while the shattered, broken, colored light from the windows lay over the pews and the bent, black-covered heads of the mourners in radiant, warm, glowing shadows.

Then we stood in that tearing, wounding wind while his body was lowered into the gray frozen ground. We stood in two separate groups, the Mexicans in their somber black, the long black veils of the women whipping in the wind like tatters of bitter flags, and that smaller group, the Jackson family. From the Mexicans rose the soft sound of weeping muffled by the folds of black shawls. The Jacksons were mute, dry-eyed, their faces as pale and gray as the light of that March day.

After it was over and we were walking to our car, I felt a hand on my arm. I turned to see Manuel's mother standing there, a small, shrunken, wizened old lady with black weeping eyes in a toothless lined face. "My little one," she said in Spanish, "this is for you. From my son, from my Manuel." And in my hand she dropped the silver medal he had worn around his neck. For many years I wore that small silver token until finally, in Barcelona, one flowery summer evening I took it from my neck and hung it around the slender brown throat of a graceful Spanish boy whose name I did not know. That was a long time ago, yet still I reach instinctively at night to touch that smooth cold silken metal when I awaken startled and frightened from those vague dreams of terror that I cannot escape.

Ah, Manuel, I gave your medal away. Foolishly, impulsively, I hung it around the neck of that beautiful boy, and I have been sorry ever since. I miss the medal. But he was very, very beautiful. Very beautiful indeed.

ENTRY IN THE DIARY OF
MARK THOMAS JACKSON,
SEPTEMBER 12, 1938

Tomorrow I leave for school. Everything is ready. My trunk was sent today. Mother sewed the last label on my clothes this afternoon, so there is nothing to do now except to go.

Funny thing, but I never really thought I would do it. It just never occurred to me to go away to school. When I think that it was only a few months ago that I was planning on buying a few sheep this fall and starting my own herd, it makes it all harder to realize. For Dad gave me sheep, and I turned them down.

I don't know if this is the right thing to do. I hate to leave Dad when things are so bad for him with his drinking so much. But Mother says that there is no way to help him, and I guess that she is right. He doesn't seem to care about things any longer.

I wonder what it will be like at St. Mark's. I shall have to study hard so Mother will not feel badly about all of her money being spent on me. I think Secoria is glad I am going. She doesn't like me. Tim likes me, though. In a way I wish I could take him with me.

I wonder if I will come back here to live again. Somehow I feel that I won't. It is a scary sort of feeling to be leaving your only home. Especially when you aren't sure you will have another. Because how could you, really? Homes are different when you are grown up. It won't be long until I am grown up. It won't be long at all.

TIMOTHY LOGAN JACKSON

Secoria insisted that I see many things I did not want to see. She took me to the pen and made me look at Mark's sheep that I already knew Mark would never claim. She pointed out to me the one lamb shivering alone, wobbling on legs too feeble to stand and bleating in a sound like that of a lost child crying for its mother. Though I neither wanted to see nor hear, Secoria made me see the lamb, and seeing it, I had to claim it.

"What is wrong with it?" I asked.

"It must be an orphan," she said. "It doesn't have a mother."

"What will happen to it?" I asked.

"It will die," she said with malicious pleasure.

I looked once more at it, feeble and weak and alone. Then I ran back toward the house. Secoria ran after me and caught me by the arm.

"Where are you going?" she said roughly, jerking me around.

"I'm going to get a bottle for that lamb," I answered, remembering that Manuel had said you could raise them on a baby bottle.

"It's not your lamb. You can't give it a bottle if Mark doesn't say you can," she said, her face dark and cruel.

"It *is* my lamb," I answered fiercely, almost desperately.

"What makes you think so?" she taunted.

"Because it is alone." I turned and ran to the house.

The lamb *was* mine without questions and without trouble because in the days that followed nobody thought about the two of us—that lamb and me. We lived out those first days quietly and alone. In a few days it was as though we had never lived separately.

Mark had been gone for four days when my lamb was lost. I kept her penned in a small pen off the corral. She had grown steadily and was now big enough to be turned out to graze, only I couldn't bear for her to go. But when I went down to feed her early one morning, before the others were awake, she was gone.

I ran back into the house, screaming for Secoria, because the sheep had to be in the pen or I couldn't bear it, because there was nobody but me for that sheep to belong to. Wasn't it an orphan? Without a mother? How much more alone could one be?

Secoria met me on the stairs.

"The lamb," I said. "My lamb. It's gone."

She looked at me, her eyes narrowed against the morning light. Then suddenly she turned and ran back up the stairs to Dad's door and began hammering on it with her fists.

"Open up," she yelled, pounding, "open up, damn you!" She beat at the door as though she were attacking an enemy.

"Secoria." Dad's voice was stern when he threw the door open. His face was pale and his eyes baggy and swollen. "Stop this noise. What's the matter with you?"

She stared right at him like she was grown and his equal, her whole body trembling with anger. She had not forgiven Dad for Manuel yet. "His lamb. Did you tell the men to take Tim's lamb to the pasture?"

He rubbed one trembling hand over his eyes for a moment. "What lamb are you talking about?" he asked tiredly.

"Tim's lamb. The one he raised. He had it penned up by the corral."

Dad looked across at me surprised, as though seeing me standing there for the first time. "Was that your lamb, Tim? I didn't know that."

Secoria began to cry then, hot bitter tears. "No, you wouldn't know that, would you? You wouldn't know anything, you drunk!" And she fled from him down the hall. He watched her until she ran into her room and slammed the door behind her. Then he turned back to me.

"I'm sorry, Tim. I sent it out to pasture. But if you want, I'll have the men bring you another one up here. I didn't know you were interested in sheep."

He looked so tired and old standing in the doorway that I could not find anything to say to him. So I turned and went back to the pen.

Mother stepped from her door as I passed it, but we neither spoke nor touched. She looked across the hall at Terrell for a moment before turning back into her room. I left the house with the three of them each locked away in a separate room.

I went out under the mesquites and cried until I had no tears left; then I lay down with my wet cheek against the warm sandy ground and slept.

Late in the afternoon I decided to go down to the double springs and throw rocks while I waited for Secoria. She had been gone all day and nobody could find her. It was almost sunset when I heard hoofbeats. I stood up on a big flat rock and watched her come riding down the path to the springs on her big horse. She was streaked with dust and dirt and there were muddy streaks across her face as though she had wiped tears away.

"Come back to the house, Timmy," she said, looking down at me. "I brought your lamb back."

It was not only that my lamb was back. It was that she went after it, that she spent a day in the saddle riding in and out among the sheep just to find that one. And she did it for me. Only for me.

I buried my face in the wool of my lamb and cried again, surprised at myself, because I had thought that there were no tears left.

X

TIMOTHY LOGAN JACKSON

Once Mark went away to school he was, for all practical purposes, out of our lives for good. Ours meaning Secoria's and mine. He never came home except for an occasional few weeks between school and camp or at Christmas.

I said he was out of our lives. Physically, yes. But actually he had simply become an inextricable part of us. He was seldom mentioned in the house; instead the family walked around his memory as though it were sacred ground. He had become for all of us the ghost from whose presence we were never completely free.

Especially Secoria. At first it seemed as though Mark's going had set her free. She laughed and sang and promptly asked Father for Mark's sheep. But Father refused. After all, Secoria was a daughter and southern girls— even though they are Texans—don't raise sheep. They wear frilly dresses and sit on the veranda and keep cool and sweet-smelling. That was what Terrell expected from his daughter. Only she couldn't understand that. Or maybe she just couldn't be that.

Instead she set about proving herself the man of the family. She was up every morning with the sun and went out with the hands, following them around, helping with the chores, learning the ways of the ranch. She rode hard, worked hard, tried hard. But it was too late as well as being the wrong thing to do.

It was too late in many ways. One, because Terrell no longer cared. For days at a time, he didn't leave his room but silently went about his drinking. And when he did come out, he spoke briefly with his foreman, then drove into town after more liquor. The foreman, a new man named Simpson, kept things going but that was all. Ranching meant nothing to him. The land held no lure, no mystery, no excitement. It was inevitable that soon the ranch should begin to show that nobody really cared, that the people who owned the land and lived on it were content to simply make their way.

Tenants, not owners. Inhabitants, not possessors. The only one who cared was a thirteen-year-old girl with nobody to show her the way. If Manuel had been alive—but he wasn't. So she struggled along as best she could.

The second reason that Secoria was too late was because Terrell could not bear to see in his daughter all the things he had longed for in his firstborn, his son and heir. It was a final irony that bore with it more pain than amusement. When he saw her riding in on her horse, covered with the dust and grime and sweat of her day, he had to turn his eyes away, for by all rights it should have been Mark coming in like that, not Secoria.

She was wrong, she was too late, but she was stubborn.

It was her stubbornness that brought on the last big battle between her and Mother. There had always been a separateness, a deep and silent hostility between the two. But it was only when Secoria reached her teens that it flared into open conflict. It came roaring into our midst and I knew, as young as I was, as frightened as I was, that it could only be settled by the defeat and exile of one of them.

Secoria used to say through clenched teeth, "I'm like my father in every way. I have nothing of my mother in me. Mark is like her, not me."

And the town would say, clucking its active tongue and wagging its disapproving head, "How did a fine woman like Hannah Jackson ever beget such a wild, outrageous girl?"

But the two Jackson women were more alike than any stranger, any casual outsider, could see. Of Hannah's three children Secoria was the one who inherited the will-like-iron, the pride-like-fire. She was the one strong enough to fight, free enough to struggle.

The adolescent Secoria gave the town of Fremond a new Jackson scandal. Not only did she wear men's clothing and try to do men's work, not only did she roam freely among the Mexican hired hands, speaking Spanish and joking carelessly, not only did she smoke in public and use words that no young lady had dared speak before, but she thumbed her nose at the town's very shock and outrage and sealed her outrageous behavior with a flare of bizarre humor. She could no longer be ignored by Hannah. One could hate Secoria, be afraid of her, long to destroy her, but one could not ignore her. That was the one thing Secoria refused: to let anybody overlook her.

"I am not going to let you continue to create a scandal, Secoria," Hannah said. "You're not going to embarrass me and mock me."

"I'm going to live my life in my own way, Mother," Secoria answered. "You can't stop me."

"Don't be too sure," Hannah said. The battle had begun.

I don't really know how she managed it, but Hannah somehow persuaded Terrell to deny Secoria the right to help on the ranch. "Young girls don't go out among working ranch hands, Secoria," he said. "You're to stay away from the men. And you're not to ride out alone anymore. Take Timmy with you."

"You know Timmy can't ride," she cried, outraged.

"I'm not going to have the Mexicans making dirty remarks about you. You're going to be a lady, Secoria, if it kills me," he said, his face flushed, his temper coming easily as it did those days.

"A lady," she said mockingly, the tears near. "A lady. You bet, Dad. I'm going to be a fine lady just like Mother." And the tears started.

"You're damn right," Terrell said, his voice hard and cold. She ran from the room, crying.

The first round went to Hannah. And the second too. Because it was Hannah who sold Secoria's horses. We came home from school on the school bus. Secoria went inside and changed her clothes. When she started out to the stable I tagged along with her because I usually helped her to saddle Lancelot and feed old Rajah. We opened the door upon the two empty stalls.

"They're gone," I said, amazed. "Do you think the boy took them out for exercise?" I asked, afraid to think what their absence meant. But Secoria stood completely still, unmoving, all the color drained from her face. Then she turned on her heel and went straight to the house. Hannah was working in the kitchen, calmly, quietly. I loved to watch her go about her work with quick deft movements. Secoria paused in the door, watching. She spoke distinctly in words as measured and sure as the competent efforts of Hannah's tireless hands. "I'll get them back, Hannah," she said.

SYE JOHN MORRISON

Well, Mark Jackson had gone off to school and Fremond had survived the Depression. Terrell had settled down to serious drinking and Hannah had become a community leader. She not only showed up every time the church opened its doors, but she could be seen moving quietly and competently behind all the town business. She led the PTA and the Ladies Community Circle. She was an election judge, even sat on the City Council. Everybody was agreed that she was a fine person, a good Christian lady and mother. There was only one problem—that girl of hers. "Did you ever see the like?" the people exclaimed. No, Fremond never had and likely never will again.

"You're like an animal what's never been tamed. And you got no more sense," I said to Secoria the day she rode that damn half-wild horse of hers up on the sidewalk in front of Cabot's. Nearly scared me out of my wits coming up on me like a hurricane. She looked over at me with those blazing eyes, tossed her hair, and said, "You're a grouch, Sye John." Then she took off as fast as she had come. No, there had never been anything quite like Secoria Jackson in Fremond.

Now there was something hard to reconcile in the images of this crazy tomboy girl and her dignified and worthy mother. Hannah had been so busy making sure Mark turned out the way she wanted him that she had overlooked the threat of this girl. By all rights Secoria should have been a quiet pleasant girl, pretty enough, smart enough, who sat with her hands neatly folded in her lap and sang in the church choir. That was the daughter for Hannah. Confronted with this outrageous rebel, there was only one thing for Hannah to do. Change her. And, being Hannah, she set to it with a will.

I remember the day she sold the horses. It must have been a year or so after Mark had gone. It was a day in early fall and I was sitting on my bench when I saw these trucks coming down the street pulling two horse trailers. John Cabot came to the door of the store and watched them pass.

"John," I said, "ain't them Secoria's horses yonder?"

"Yessir, they sure are," he answered, blinking his eyes and smiling in that way he has that durn near turns your blood cold. It's one of them smiles that ain't got a damn bit of humor in it. "Hannah told me she was selling them. Good riddance, too. That girl would have broken her fool neck on 'em."

"You got work to do inside, John Cabot," I said.

It was near sunset when I started toward the boarding house. I had stayed at the bench longer than usual because I had been expecting— what, I don't know for sure. But something. I knew that the girl would do something.

I had made it halfway up the street when she called to me. She was riding in some broken-down truck driven by a Mexican and she jumped out before he could even stop good.

"Sye John," she called, running up to me, "you saw them, didn't you? You must have seen them pass the store."

"I saw them," I answered.

"Did you recognize the trucks?" she asked. Her face was pale and hard, composed. She looked like her mother. Her face had that same masklike look that I had seen on Hannah's.

"Burnet Stockyards, I think. Looked like their trucks to me. 'Course I don't see none too good."

She stood for a moment, thinking. "Burnet," she said softly. "I can catch a ride on the highway." And she started off in that direction.

"Secoria," I said, calling to her, "don't make me run after you with this peg leg. You wait up a minute."

"Go on home, Sye John," she said, never even slowing down.

"How you gonna get 'em back without money?" I was having to durn near shout because she was so far away by this time.

"Steal them!" she yelled, and she began to run. There wasn't nothing I could do except stand there and watch her go. When she was out of sight I went on my way back to the boarding house.

In the hall I met the landlady. "Mrs. Malone," I said, "you better call up Hannah Jackson and tell her to go get her daughter off the highway before she gets runned over."

"What's that fool girl doing out on the highway?" Mrs. Malone asked, already on her way to the telephone. She didn't wait for me to answer, just kept talking like she does. "That child needs a firm hand, that's what she needs."

Terrell picked her up off the highway and took her home. She didn't get her horses back either. Instead she took to driving automobiles.

LETTER FROM GREGORY TREMAYNE
TO HIS FATHER, MOFFETT TREMAYNE,
WRITTEN NOVEMBER 10, 1960

Dear Dad,

Tony got me out of bed today by sheer brute force. He made me dress and eat breakfast and walked with me to Simmons Hall where I have my first class. But it didn't do any good. Because I walked in one door of the building and out another. Then I went to the post office and found your letter. I spent the rest of the morning at a place called the Coffee Mill because they don't care how long you sit and stare into space and also because it is warm and quiet there.

About lunchtime good ole Tony came in looking for me. One of my friends had told him that I didn't make it inside the classroom and he came after me. Lately I spend lots of time at this coffee place so it wasn't hard for him to find me. He sat down, looked at me and said, "For Christ's sake, Greg, what's eating you?"

He's a good guy, Tony is. A really good guy. He is sincere and concerned and honest and upright and conscientious and bright and hardworking—in every way a really good guy. Only I am sick to death of him. And bored with him. And don't really give a damn about him. That's not a very easy thing to admit—that your best friend leaves you cold. But he does and that's that.

So I said to him, "Tony, did I tell you about the time I went down to the train station and saw a whale that was in a boxcar? A sure enough whale traveling through Texas in a boxcar. At the stations the trainmen let the kids get on to see it. A dead whale."

But Tony is a good serious guy. He just sat there and quietly asked, "What in the hell is wrong with you? You aren't heading for the funny farm, are you?" Which is the accepted way of hinting that somebody might be having a nervous breakdown.

"No," I said, "I'm heading for Europe."

"Like hell," Tony said. He is a very practical young man, Tony is, and will make a good accountant, which is what he intends to be.

This brings me to the point of this letter. You mentioned earlier that I might be allowed a trip to Europe this summer. I wondered if I might go now since it is doing me no good to be here in school if I cannot make myself study or care about studying. All I do is wander around looking at things and remembering things like that whale (that did happen, didn't it? Or did I just dream it when I was a kid?) and what Secoria Jackson was like when I first knew her.

Only there isn't much to look at in this little town and nothing that I haven't seen before. In Europe I could at least see something different even if I have to keep all my tired old memories.

Besides, a son who is a bum in Europe will sound better to Mother's bridge club than a son who is a bum in Iowa. So if you could let me go now, I would appreciate it.

Seriously, Dad, I need to go somewhere. Please give it some thought.

Love,
Greg

SYE JOHN MORRISON

It was about three weeks after the horse-selling incident before I saw Secoria again. And this time I had to look hard to be sure that my eyes weren't failing me. For here came this young girl swishing along down the sidewalk in one of them full-skirted dresses what has them rustling petticoats under it. She had long reddish hair like Secoria, but instead of it falling all over her face it was brushed and tied back with a blue ribbon. Still, there was something about the way the girl walked, some long-striding, no-nonsense way that told me it had to be Secoria. She might be wearing a fancy dress but she hadn't learned how to handle it yet. She came striding along like she had on a dusty pair of blue jeans.

She came right up to the bench and sat down. She stared at me for a minute and finally said, "Well?"

"Well, nothing," I said.

"What do you think about me as a lady?"

"I think you got too much paint on." She not only had her hair brushed, but her cheeks were glowing a bright red and her lips which were full and sort of pouty had on enough of that lip rouge for two women. Actually she looked rather pathetic sitting there with her face thin and freckled under the paint. Like some kid who has been playing in her mother's belongings. I felt sort of sorry for her having to grow up and not quite sure how it was done. "You look right nice though," I said.

"The hell I do," she said, tossing her head.

Now her face may have still seemed young, a kid's face, but the dress revealed something mighty different. It fit tight around the top with a low neck, and it sort of cried out that the wearer was no longer a child. It was the kind of dress that was meant to advertise that very fact.

"Did Hannah buy you that dress?" I asked. I had seen Secoria before in school clothes, skirts and blouses and things like that. But this dress was something different. It was more grown up. An obvious sort of dress, if you know what I mean.

"No," she said triumphantly. "I bought it myself. Dad said I could. After all, the money from the horses belongs to me." She turned and looked at me with those blazing, angry eyes.

"Well, it's quite a dress," I said, feeling sorry for her because she had such a load of anger and hurt and bewilderment and hatred to carry and the only thing she knew to do with it was to blaze out in some sort of flashy way.

"That's why I bought it," she said. Then she leaned back on the bench and waited. Only she didn't have to wait long before one of the MacEvern boys came by and saw her there. He stopped and looked with his mouth open.

Finally he said, "What you doing all dressed up like that, Secoria?"

"Like what?" she said, just daring him to go on.

"I don't know," he said. "I just mean, you look too dressed up to be sitting here on this bench with Sye John. And beside, it's not much like you."

"How do you know what's like me?" she asked, only her voice was low, soft, and she was smiling up at him. I couldn't believe it. Here she was making like a coquette who had never in her life tried it before. And she wasn't doing too bad either.

"Well," the boy said, blushing and shuffling his feet, "I guess I really don't know." He stood there for a little while embarrassed. "You like to have a soda?" he asked finally.

"I think that might be nice," she said, and got up from the bench with a great rustle of petticoats and a wafting of perfume. "You be good now," she said to me with a wave of her hand as they moved off down the sidewalk. But the Secoria who had Ben MacEvern flushed and admiring didn't have me fooled one bit. Because I had seen her eyes as she said goodbye and they were as hard and angry as ever. Just a little amused, maybe.

Lord God in heaven, I said to myself as they walked off. For if Hannah had thought she had trouble before, it was nothing to what she was going to have now.

MOFFETT TREMAYNE

When I returned to Fremond after the Depression I was amazed to find how the town had changed. It seemed to have shrunk, to have tightened up like the skin on an old man's face will seem to tighten around the bones, making the whole face and head seem smaller and narrower. Of course I was old enough to know that it was not the town that had changed so much as it was that I had changed. I had gone out into the world a little and seen a few things. I had watched some of the changes that were going on in the nation, had read of the changes going on in the world. In the light of all this, Fremond's very changelessness seemed to reduce it, to diminish it.

During the war years I was away from Fremond again. For a while I was in Washington, then out on the West Coast, and finally back in Texas at Fort Hood. It was convenient being close to Fremond. I could come home every few weeks to see Emmaline and Greg. And every time I made that trip there was once again the little shock of amazement at finding how untouched the town was. Half the world could go up in flames and Fremond still drowsed in the sun, Sye John still sat on his bench in front of Cabot's store. Except for an occasional uniform on the street or a glimpse of a star hanging in the window of a house, there was no sign of the war.

I was packing for a trip home when Nick Rankin stopped in the door of my room. He was a young captain who lived next room to mine in the BOQ.

"It must be nice to be going home for the weekend," he said wistfully.

"It is," I answered without looking up. Rankin was a nice guy, but I really didn't know him too well. He was a quiet boy who had seen action in Europe. He had been injured there, had been sent back here to wait out the war. He was tall and slender with a peculiar way of walking. He seemed to favor his left leg as though it were not too reliable or strong. A memory of his wound perhaps.

"God, I'd like to go home for the weekend," he said.

"Where you from, Rankin?" I asked.

"Connecticut."

"Small town?"

"Yes. About thirty thousand."

"Hell, man, that's a city," I said, laughing. "My town has about six thousand." I put the shirt I was holding into the bag, then I looked across the suitcase at Rankin. "You've been home in the past year, haven't you?" I asked him.

"Yes. I had a leave when I got out of the hospital. Before I came here."

"How was it in your town? Any changes?"

"Changes?"

"I mean since the war."

"Christ, yes. They've built a defense plant there. The town's full of new people."

"You have a weekend pass, Rankin?"

"Yeah. Thought I'd go into Waco."

"Why don't you come home with me? I can show you a town that never seems to change."

And so I brought Nick Rankin to Fremond.

Nick and I took a walk down the main street of Fremond.

"One thing about it," I said to Nick, "it's not like New England."

In front of Cabot's store we met Terrell and Secoria Jackson.

"Well, Moffett," Terrell said, "you look right dashing in that uniform."

I introduced Nick to the Jacksons, noticing the contrast between the tall young man in his crisp khaki and the rancher in his old faded levis. "I'm showing Mr. Rankin the glories of our fair city."

"Where's your home, Captain?" Terrell asked.

"Connecticut."

"You've never seen ranching country before?" Terrell asked.

"This is my first time."

"Bring him out to Turkey Bend, Moffett," Terrell said. "It's the only decent ranch around here." Then he and the girl moved off down the sidewalk.

"Terrell's family has been here since this town began," I said to Nick as we stood watching after them. "Turkey Bend is an old ranch and a good one if you'd be interested in seeing it."

"How old is she?" he asked. I looked at him, surprised. Then I saw that he was watching Secoria, that she was all he had seen.

"Well," I said, "she must be about seventeen." I hadn't realized that Secoria was that old. She's grown up, I thought.

"She's lovely," Nick said.

We went to Turkey Bend that afternoon at Nick's request. Only we weren't going to see the ranch.

TERRELL L. JACKSON

To tell the truth, I was glad when that young captain started coming to Fremond to see Secoria. Sure, he was older, but he seemed like a nice sort of young man. I thought that he might be just what Secoria needed—someone older and more levelheaded to control her. Her mother and I weren't doing so well at it.

It was hard for me to see just how it had happened, but somewhere along the way Secoria and I had become lost from each other and no matter how hard I tried to reach her, she never seemed to hear or understand a word I said. I watched her becoming more and more rebellious, more and more desperate, but I knew of no way to help her for I could not even help myself.

She had left her tomboy years behind, but what had replaced them was something harder to handle. For one thing she had turned into quite a beauty. Not the gentle quiet sort but one of those overripe, flaming girls— all soft curves and flashing eyes. She was the type of woman who attracted men, lots of men. And this new power she had discovered did not cause her to suddenly develop new poise and dignity as happens with many beautiful women. Instead it gave her a weapon.

Yes, I thought Nick Rankin would be good for her. He was a gentle quiet man with dignity and a nice sort of humor. The first time he came to the ranch I had thought that Secoria would get rid of him in a hurry. He didn't seem like the type she would be interested in. She had always seemed to favor the flashier sort of male, one of those men with plenty of money to throw around, a fast car, a loud laugh.

When she came home from her first evening out with Rankin she stopped by the living room. I had trouble sleeping so I was still up, sitting alone. Usually she passed by the room without speaking to me, so I was surprised when she came in. She sat down across from me without speaking. We sat together for a while, silent.

"Well," I finally said, too loud, too heartily, "did you have a good time with that Yankee soldier?"

"Yes," she said. "He's a very nice person, Terrell." She hesitated a moment, then went on. "You know what word I keep thinking of when he is around? Complete. That's how he seems to me, as though there is nothing missing in his life, as though he's never been maimed or diminished in any way." She smiled at me. "I didn't know there could be people like that."

"I'm not sure there can be," I answered.

We sat together for a while, not talking, simply sitting among the shadows. Finally she got up to leave and walked to the door. There she hesitated, turned around and came back to my chair. Bending over swiftly, she kissed me lightly on the cheek. "Good night, Daddy," she said.

Yes, I was glad that Nick Rankin had come along. It was about time Secoria had somebody she could depend on. She had never had that before.

SECORIA JACKSON

I loved Nick Rankin.

It was during the war and Nick Rankin was a tall, blond, slightly stooped man who walked with a limp. He was soft-spoken and gentle; yet he was the first man I had known who could not be shocked, frightened, or bullied by me. He was a man to whom the world had proportion and order, who never woke up crying in the night. A man that a war could not twist or change.

It was, in every way, an unlikely romance. I was seventeen and still in high school. Nick was twenty-three. He had left college his junior year to enlist in the army, had fought in Europe and been wounded. He was a New Englander; I had never seen the Atlantic Ocean. There was no logical explanation for the fact that I loved him, that for eight months I waited only for his voice, his smile, his touch.

When I discovered that I was pregnant it seemed to me a wonderful thing. I was neither frightened nor ashamed because I loved and believed in Nick. I will marry him, I thought, and soon the war will be over. We'll go home then to that town of clapboard houses sitting solidly among green lawns, to that world of gentle ways and reticent strong people that produced my Nick.

Not that he had said anything about taking me. But I knew that he would because I could not imagine living without him. I was safe with him; I couldn't afford to let him go.

Then I got the letter. It was a nice letter, friendly and brief. Nick had gotten transferred (he had forgotten to mention to me that he had applied) and was leaving. He was sorry that he couldn't get to Fremond to say good-bye, but he wanted me to know that he would always remember the time we had spent together. I was the only thing that had made his stay in Texas tolerable. It was a nice letter of dismissal.

There was nothing for me to do except go to Terrell. The next day I told him that I was pregnant and that I wanted to go away. Terrell took me in his arms and cried, hoarsely, roughly, the way a man cries. I wanted to cry with him, I wanted to put my arms around him, to comfort and be comforted, but I could only stand still and unyielding in the circle of his arms.

Terrell and Hannah made the arrangements and I went to stay with a woman in San Antonio. There was a doctor there who handled the affair very discreetly. I never saw my child, but they told me that it was a boy.

Did I say *my* child? No, it was not mine, nor was he yours, Nick Rankin. We only gave him life; we never loved nor claimed him.

I did not return to Fremond again until Mother's final illness. And now I will never go back again.

When Hannah left me in San Antonio she leaned forward and kissed me on the cheek. I drew back quickly and said to her, "Go on home, Mother, where you can pray for my soul." She answered me in her soft voice, "I pray for all of us, Secoria. All of us."

Hannah prayed for us, Terrell wept for us, but it didn't do any good either way.

XI

GREGORY TREMAYNE

I spent the morning wandering in the graveyard, running my fingers over the marble and granite stones. Some of the stones are smooth and cool; others are rough with little sharp edges protruding from the surface. On some of the stones, the ones that have been in the ground for a long time, there is a sort of moss growing, a wet soft growth that feels like velvet, only damp. I do not know what draws me to that graveyard these days. At least I don't know exactly. For a while I thought it might be the peace of the place. Somehow it is as though the very air inside the walls is different. Stiller, somehow. Unstirred by breathing. The trees and flowers, the path and graves are all orderly and lovely, like a formal garden where nobody is ever seen walking or working but which is always perfect with the grass the exact same length and with the dead leaves carefully pruned away.

I like the angels best. They are lovely creatures with soft blind faces and weather marks on their cheeks like tear stains. There is one of them whose face is hidden. She is a large angel, bigger than a human, and she is kneeling with her arms covering her head. One side of her stone garment has slipped down over her outflung arms and you can see the curve of a womanly breast. She is a sorrowing angel, grieving over a grave marked with only one word—LORACK.

Maybe I go to the graveyard because it is peaceful and quiet, because there are no demands made there on anybody or by anybody and therefore not any demands on me to think or be or do. Or maybe it is because I can feel the past there, caught inside those pink stone walls. It is as though the air, the trees, the flowers, even the stone angels are all only memories caught there, unmoving. There is no time there, no change, no coming and going. Only the past and not the past active. But the past stilled and dead, quiet and complete. Over. Finished.

And that is what I want to know. Is the past over and finished? Is it ever done and complete and how and why? Or is it all we have and are our lives nothing but memories and is living somehow a tying together and reinterpreting, an attempting to understand what is past and how do you live with the past and triumph over it or do you or should you and most importantly how do you grasp it within your hands and what is it? What is it? What is my past and where in it did I begin?

I remember my first funeral. It was when Timothy Jackson was buried. I asked to go to the funeral because I knew Timothy and he was the first person I had ever known who had died. I wanted to see what the difference was between Timothy Present and Timothy Past. I had known the Timothy Present. I wanted to see what it was that went away and made Timothy Past. Mother said I was too young but Father had said, Let him go. It was in the fall, a gray melancholy day with the air still a little heavy with the last summer heat. A dusty day, uncertain of itself. No longer summer, yet hesitant about plunging into winter with its long silences and bleak light. The church had been too warm. My collar was tight and I felt choked, both by the collar and by the heavy odor of flowers that hung unreal and almost tangible on the air. The body was in a dark casket at the front of the church. Mrs. Jackson sat near the front with her face hidden by a black veil. Her husband sat on one side of her, and Mark, just home from the war, on the other. Secoria was not there. And I sat there, knowing suddenly what it meant to be Timothy Past. It meant not having your collar choke you and not smelling the flowers and not seeing the faces of the people and not feeling the fall day around you. It meant being in a box away from everything and yet somehow being a part of everything because it had taken all the past to make you and now you were with the past that had produced you.

Father asked me if I wanted to go to the graveyard, but I had said no, burying my face against him because I was so terribly sad. Not for Tim and not for the Jacksons, but for myself.

TERRELL L. JACKSON

I have always been afraid of judging and never quite knew how to do it. Maybe that has been my fatal flaw: to never be able to know or say, This is The One and Only Way. This is The Right. I knew what I wanted and I lived on action. This I desire so this I will grab. And when I grabbed and could not reach, when I acted and my act ended in impotence or in some result that I had not sought, I was bewildered and could not say what had gone wrong. I could not look back and judge between what might have been and what was. Everything merged and became One, the Inconvertible, the Inseparable. It wasn't that I felt What Is, Is Right, but more, What Is, Is.

That is why, try as I might, I can never understand how Tim, my beloved and unknown son, could take his own life. I cannot understand how he chose, how he weighed life and death and judged one to be more adequate than the other. I cannot understand how he judged himself and found himself either unfit for life, or else more fitted for death. Of course, I remember certain things, certain traits of his or events that give me some sort of clue as to what may have influenced him. But before the understanding of his act, I stand helpless.

I have stumbled along in this world, blind and fumbling, but I have never doubted myself to be part of it. I don't believe that Tim ever felt himself to belong to the world or to life. Not that he didn't try. My God, how he tried! But he always tried with the sort of desperation that knows before it begins that it is doomed to failure. The kind of action that cries out hysterically, I am going through these motions because I must, but I do not understand them or their purpose.

There was the time of the shearing. It was in the spring of 1945, and men were scarce as they had been all during the war. I had been as far south as McAllen looking for help and still was shorthanded. Tim had come to me timidly and offered to help. I was surprised at his gesture. And

169

then surprised at my own surprise. For he was, after all, fifteen years old. Certainly that was old enough to go out shearing. I had taken Mark with me since he was about ten years old. But it had never occurred to me to take Tim.

Maybe it was because he was small for his age, a slight boy who suffered from asthma. A boy who was in no way suited for ranching or for hard work. Maybe it was because I so seldom thought of him in any way. At any rate, I was surprised at his offer to help. And touched.

We went out early with the few men I had been able to gather. "You'd better watch for a while to see what happens," I said. He watched the first three sheep, heard them bleating helplessly, saw them get up and run away from the shears with the blood flowing from the nicks and cuts. Then he went over into the bushes and was sick. He did not say a word to me but simply turned and began the long walk back to the ranchhouse. We never mentioned the incident to each other.

It was not long after that day that he approached Hannah with the idea of going away to school at St. Mark's, as Mark had done. She came to me and said, "I don't think he should go. He's not strong enough or well enough to be able to stand the strain of going away to school."

"I think it might be good for him," I said. "He's a smart kid. He does well in his studies. Actually he is more of a scholar than Mark."

"It's hard enough for him to live here where he is protected by his family," she answered, her eyes sad and old. She was aging rapidly now. "I don't think he could stand the strain of a strange place."

"It might not be as strange or trying a place as his own home," I said, rising to the occasion of a talk between Hannah and me with my own brand of sarcasm and bitterness.

But she didn't seem to notice. "He misses Secoria," she said.

We did not allow him to go off to school, partly because we somehow knew that he was trying to follow Mark, to be like Mark. We felt that we were saving him the pain of failing again, as he had failed at the shearing. For who could be like Mark? Who could supplant Mark, the son, the heir?

Then the war ended and Mark was coming home. Hannah looked younger and less worn. Her cheeks were faintly pink from the anticipation of her son's coming in the door, coming back from the war whole and a man. I was excited too, for I felt that when he came back, he might want to stay. Perhaps he would have decided that he needed the ranch and the ranch needed him. I remembered how I had felt when I came back from the First War, more eager to see my land than to see my father. I remembered how I had dreamed of my home and of the ranch all those nights I had spent in France, and I thought that it might be that way with Mark.

The night before Mark was to arrive the next day, Tim came into the room where I was working on the ranch accounts. "I wanted to tell you good night, Dad," he said.

"Good night, son. Sleep well," I said automatically, hardly glancing at him. He stopped by Hannah's room to say good night, then went to his own room. Twenty minutes later he was dead. My youngest son, unknown and scarcely thought about, had hanged himself. He had weighed himself in some unknown scale and found himself wanting.

SYE JOHN MORRISON

Fremond was changed by the Depression. Diminished, you might say. But it was shriveled by the war. There are more casualties come out of a war than are listed in the records and there are more places destroyed than ever see a battle.

Just take the case of old Sye John, for instance. You might say that this Second World War did me in. Because what it did was exhaust my mind. It changed so many things in so many ways that I can't even grasp it all. And it messed up my whole world without my ever leaving Fremond or catching sight of a German or a Jap.

Maybe I was just too old to take it all in. And maybe I was just too narrow. Probably it was both. For a long time I had looked at my little world without thinking or worrying about what happened outside this town. Then a war started over in Europe and then out in the Pacific Ocean and the tremors from all them bombs and guns and airplanes split my town like some durn earthquake. And while I could see the damage that was done, I couldn't always understand it because I couldn't see how it began or understand all that was involved. It was like the war tilted my town enough off center to take lots of things out of focus. And I've never been able to get it all straight again. Things moved too fast in that damn war for an old man with a peg leg to keep up.

So I tried not to notice the war or think about it too much. I talked about it, sure. But my talking didn't mean anything. I just said the same damn things everybody said. When I read the papers I didn't even try to get the meaning of all that was happening and being said. I simply tried to think of it as some kind of game; I looked upon it as trying to see who was ahead in the scoring. That was all my mind was up to.

Yet I could see the changes here in Fremond. Boys going away to be killed with some of them coming back mangled in body and lots of them coming back mangled in spirit and all of them coming back different with

172

eyes full of new places and new ideas. It wasn't like the First War. Then the men came back like they was coming home. Like they wanted to forget what happened, put it all behind them. Then it was like they wanted to return as quickly as possible to the way things had been before they left. But this second time the young men came home different. Restless, somehow. Like they knew that the war wasn't really over yet. Like they knew that things never would be the same again. And God knows they haven't been. At least not for old men, narrow men, peg-legged men.

No, I tried not to pay any more attention to the war than I absolutely had to. Instead I kept watching my same old street, trying to figure out what was happening here under my nose. That was enough to keep me busy.

I used to sit here every day and watch the people coming and going to the post office. That was one of the big changes the war made in Fremond. The post office, which had always been important, became the very lifeline of the town. People who had never done more than send off an order to Sears Roebuck suddenly began marking the day by the mail coming in, waiting for a letter from their son. Mothers and young girls sent packages and snapshots and received presents from far-off places like England and Paris and Tokyo. Yessir, you might say that the post office came into its own.

But there was one person who went to the post office every day for a special reason that had nothing to do with the war. That was Tim Jackson. Every day he would ride up in front of the post office on his bicycle. He would go in and mail a letter to his sister. And every day he would come back out and climb on his bicycle to ride away empty-handed. For she never answered one of them.

And then, when the war was over and before enough of the young men got home to show us that the town was not ever going to be the same and while we still had the belief that it really was All Over, Tim Jackson killed himself.

SECORIA JACKSON

In the fall of 1945 I was safely enrolled in San Pedros Female Academy. I had given birth to a child which I had never seen, I had left my home for good, I had loved a man who had left me. Pretty impressive for eighteen years, no matter how one considers it.

And I was dead set on forgetting all of it. I did not want to think about Fremond or my family or my brothers or Nick. I especially did not want to think about that child that I had carried and had felt moving within me and that I had loved even before it was born. That child that I had brought living into the world and had surrendered to another woman's arms without once seeing its little face. I wanted most to forget that formless face that I dreamed of every night and could never quite manage to see.

I was determined to forget. So I burned all the letters that came from home except those from Terrell. I could count on him to write only the facts that I needed to know, letters that were confined to business and enclosed money. The letters that I could not allow myself to read were from Tim. Because if I read them I would have to remember too many things. How the ranch looked, how Tim and I had played together, how we loved each other and clung together even when we were still babies. When one is forgetting one must be merciless, for the least bit of self-indulgence, the least luxury of old love, will pull one back into the pit of all that is past. So I burned the letters from my brother. Letters that may have contained pleas for help. And when he had no hope left, he wrote me one last letter. When Terrell found his body the letter was lying on his desk unsigned.

I shall, no doubt, forget everything else that has happened to me. I am quite an expert at forgetting now. But Tim will always be with me, the evergreen memory, the undying ghost.

THE LAST LETTER OF
TIMOTHY LOGAN JACKSON, WRITTEN
TO HIS SISTER ON SEPTEMBER 11, 1945

Dear Secoria,

I have written you every day even though you do not write to me and I know that you don't read my letters. But it helped me to write them to you. I know that you are mixed up and unhappy because things have been so bad for you. Please believe me that they will be better. I know that they will because you are a tough person. You've been able to stand a lot. You won't ever have to worry about finding a place for yourself in this world because you are the kind of wonderful human being who can make a place for yourself.

Sis, I am not that kind of person. I can't seem to find any place where I belong nor anybody that I belong to. And I don't have any idea how to go about making a place for myself. It is a very lonely life to always be by yourself and afraid and confused. It is so lonely that I really don't think I can stand it anymore. I want you to understand that it is not because I feel there is anything wrong with the way you have acted about the letters. I know you have only done what you had to do. Believe me, this has nothing to do with anybody but myself. It is just that I have never understood how to go about living. I hope you understand. I do not want you to worry or to be sorry about me.

With all my love

XII

ENTRY IN THE DIARY OF MARK THOMAS JACKSON, JUNE 18, 1946

Tomorrow I shall be ordained a minister and a servant of the Most High God and His Holy Church. It is a frightening responsibility. And yet I am sure that it is the right thing. It is the profession that I am best suited for and also the one that is best suited for me. I have seen and known enough of suffering and misunderstanding in my life. Only in and through the church can I find the sort of harmony and order which can give meaning to life. That has been proved to me by the example of my own family. Only my mother, with her strong religious faith, has been able to build any sort of worthy life.

Tomorrow will be a big day for Mother. I guess it will be the first happy day she has had in several years. I hope that Dad will not spoil it for her. She has had more than her share of worries over him and Secoria and even poor Tim. Surely she deserves this one day of peace. I wonder how she will feel watching this ordination that she dreamed of even before I was born.

NELLIE BARTON

One of the most glorious days I have been allowed to witness in our church was the day Mark Jackson was ordained into the ministry. Now that was some service, I'm here to tell you! The church was packed with people because we had never had one of our own boys become a preacher before. And then, lots of people came because they were so happy for Hannah Jackson. That poor woman had had so many bad things happen to her that it was a relief to be in on one good thing.

It was a fine service too. I never saw a better-looking young man than Mark Jackson nor one that had any better manners. All the preachers from neighboring towns along with some from the seminary came to assist in the service. Some of the ladies in town fixed the church up with flowers and things were really nice, if I do say so myself.

As for Hannah, she sat up close to the front dressed all in black. She still wore mourning for Tim although he had been dead for almost a year. Well, she may have been dressed in black, but her face was shining. Simply shining. It was like I told Myra Cabot. "Myra," I said, "there is a woman that has come into her glory. And about time, too." Because it was common knowledge in this town that anything good came out of that Jackson bunch was because of Hannah and not because of Terrell.

Oh it was a fine day, I tell you. A fine day for everybody.

SYE JOHN MORRISON

You want to hear a sad story? Well, I can sure tell one. I can tell you one that will durn near make you cry. And it causes a special sort of sadness. Because it's a story that seems so little and petty and meaningless.

You see, Mark Jackson came back from the war all grown up. He was a handsome lad, full of confidence and good manners and winning ways. He went off to the seminary and begin to study to be a preacher just like Hannah had always intended for him to do. He left the week after Tim's funeral. Well, I thought, that's that. It seemed that everything was pretty well settled out at Turkey Bend Ranch. Hannah kept busy with her church and civic work, Terrell kept busy with his drinking. Tim was dead, Secoria in Washington working as a secretary, and Mark studying to be a preacher. Everything all totaled up. Then came Mark's ordination and the last pitiful postscript added to the story.

It seems like the church got together and done its durnedest to make that ordination service something fine. Maybe it was making up to Hannah for that incident years before. Or maybe it was just because a small town don't turn out too many preachers. At any rate, nearly everybody dressed up and went to see Mark made into a man of God. Nearly everybody except Terrell Jackson.

That's the pitiful part of the story—that Terrell Jackson who had known for years that he had lost any chance with Mark couldn't rise above his own disappointment and let the boy go in peace and dignity. No, Terrell had to make an ugly little scene for himself and for the boy. Actually he probably did it out of some perverse desire to hurt Hannah. But the reasons don't really matter too much. The deed is all that can be reckoned. And it was a sad, meaningless act.

It seems that he sat out at the ranch drinking, not bothering to go to the service. Then, when the service was over and Mark and Hannah came out of the church with the ministers who had conducted the service, he was waiting for them dressed in his dusty work clothes, unshaven, drunk. Mark rose right to the occasion, I'll say that for the boy. He walked over to his dad and took his arm. "Dad," he said, "I would like for you to meet some gentlemen." But Terrell was drunk, like I said. He pulled away and turned on the boy.

"I ain't interested in any goddamn preachers," he said. "And I ain't interested in you either." With that he pulled his arm back and aimed a punch at Mark. Only, being drunk and all, he didn't do too well. His fist only grazed the boy's chin and Terrell lost his balance. He fell to the ground. Mark hesitated only a second, then he bent and helped his father up. "Come on, Dad, let's go home," he said softly.

He led Terrell to the pickup, the big man leaning against him. I'll never forget the sight of the two of them going there between the rows of people all grown still and quiet. The boy tall and serious in his black suit, the father weeping against him in the way a drunk can cry. And behind them came Hannah, her head high, her face set in that stony way that didn't betray a single feeling.

To my way of thinking that is as sad a story as ever I've told.

ENTRY IN THE DIARY OF
MARK THOMAS JACKSON,
NOVEMBER 10, 1960

Today my father and I spoke about my ordination—something which I had always hoped would never be mentioned between us. It was after dinner. We had taken a walk together down to the double springs where we sat together in the faint hazy light of early evening watching the springs bubbling the water to the surface, and then following the course of the water as it trickled over the rocks and down through the draw. We had been sitting in silence when suddenly Dad said softly, "I've been meaning to apologize to you for some time, Mark. I want you to know that I was wrong and that I am deeply sorry."

I knew what he meant, of course. He didn't have to mention the incident. It had hung between us for years, putting a strain on every meeting, everything we said to each other.

"It's all right," I said.

But he wanted to talk. "You see, Mark," he said, "I simply didn't understand. I somehow felt that you were becoming a preacher just to suit your mother. I couldn't stand to think you were pleasing her when you could have been pleasing me." His mouth twisted in a wry smile. Then he said, "You have a lot to forgive me for, Mark. I hope that you can."

I looked at him sitting there in that dim light. He's an old man with gray hair and hands that shake when he lights his cigarette. His face is lined and shrunken with traces of broken veins on the cheekbones and nose and his eyes are infinitely sad.

"I'll forgive you, Dad, if you can forgive me," I said.

He smiled and put his hand on my arm. "In the long run, son, that is all that can ever be said between a parent and a child."

I wish that I had told him the truth. I did become a minister because I wanted to please Mother. And because it was a way of life that I could handle, in which I could be successful. I did not have a faith that would not let me rest without speaking, no celestial voice called me out. No, I became a minister because it seemed the easiest path for the young man that I was to accomplish the things I wanted to accomplish.

I have served honestly and faithfully and worked hard. But all these years I have felt a strange lack in me. I remember the way Mother was, her total commitment to her faith. And I remember how Dad loved his ranch. And I wonder how it would be to care so much, to have something mean so much that it dominates you and fills your life.

Tomorrow I am going back to Memphis and to my work. I will pray tonight for tolerance and understanding and strength. I will also pray for forgiveness. May we all forgive each other and may the Most High God forgive us all.

LETTER FROM MOFFETT TREMAYNE
TO HIS SON, GREGORY,
WRITTEN NOVEMBER 12, 1960

Dear Greg,

I have thought a great deal about your letter and your request. And I have decided to let you go to Europe now. Your mother and I discussed the matter last night and, after a few tears, she agreed. Now, son, it is up to you. I would suggest that you cancel your registration at school so that you may leave without flunking all your courses. Then we would like for you to come home for a few days' visit before you go. We could help you plan your trip. However, this is not a condition that you have to meet. It may be that you would like to handle everything from where you are and leave immediately. If this is the case, then you may. Like I said, it is up to you.

I could tell you that what you are looking for is not to be found in Europe any more than it is to be found in Fremond, but you wouldn't listen. Besides, that is something that you have to discover on your own, I suppose. I am sending money to underwrite your expenses for at least three months if you are frugal. As your mother and I had planned to give you this trip for a graduation present, we already had the money set aside.

It is a funny thing, Greg, but even as I write this I see you in my mind as you were ten years ago when you had freckles and went barefooted. It is hard for me to realize that you are grown up now. What does a man say to his grown-up son? I can only think of God bless you.

With love,
Father

LETTER FROM GREGORY TREMAYNE
TO HIS FATHER, MOFFETT TREMAYNE,
WRITTEN NOVEMBER 14, 1960

Dear Dad,

Thanks for everything. Thanks for the money and for the freedom to decide and for the patience and for the understanding and for everything. As you guessed, I would rather handle the plans by myself and leave from here without coming home.

I have looked into matters and have things pretty well planned out. In two weeks I should be able to get under way. Things have gone well here at the school. I was able to drop out without any trouble. If I should decide to come back, it will make things easier.

I am planning on going to England first and I will see what develops from there. I want to travel free and easy. Sort of follow my instincts. I believe that will be the best way for me. I'll see Secoria in London, Brian in Paris, and everything else I can. Tell Sye John I'll mail him a postcard of the Eiffel Tower. As to coming home, Dad, I will when I think I can. That may be a long time.

But I know that no matter where I go or for how long I shall never really get away from Fremond. This much I have already learned.

Please soothe everything over with Mother about the trip.

I don't want her to worry. I am going to be all right.

And once again, thank you.

Love,
Greg

P.S. It is all right to think of me as barefooted and freckle-faced. That's how I think of myself.

SYE JOHN MORRISON

There's only one train a morning that stops here. It's a slow train on its way to Austin. I don't reckon it will be stopping here much longer because it don't seem like there's many what wants to get on or off here at Fremond. Railroads ain't so important as they used to be. People nowadays can travel in their own automobile. And towns like Fremond ain't so important either. People are rushing off to the cities.

But there was a passenger to get on that train this morning. Mark Jackson, going over to Austin to catch a plane back to Memphis. He's been living there for two, three years now. Ever since they made him a bishop. He and Terrell came riding by this morning in Terrell's old truck. When I saw them two fine suitcases in the back I knew that Mark was on his way back to his work.

After the train pulled out of the station, Terrell came driving up the street. When he got even with my bench he pulled his truck over and stopped. Then he got out and came up to the bench to sit down.

"Well, Sye John," he said, lighting his cigarette, "my boy's gone back to Memphis."

"I figured as much," I said. We sat there for a while and looked out over the street.

"Hannah used to always say, 'I wonder what Sye John can see from that bench of his,'" Terrell said.

"Just the main street of Fremond, Texas, Terrell. Nothing more than that."

"That ain't much, Sye John."

"I reckon it's enough."

He dropped his cigarette on the ground and rubbed it out with his toe. "I guess I should be getting on home," he said, "but there's that damn empty house to face. You know, Sye John, it's a funny feeling when they are all finally gone."

He sat there thinking about the house where he had taken Hannah as a bride, where the children had grown up. That house that had seen so much and sheltered so much and now was empty and still.

"What does a man do when he gets old?" he asked me.

"He sits," I said. "He remembers. There ain't too much else left to him."

Then he got up from the bench. "I guess I'd better be getting on back," he said. He walked to the truck and climbed in, started the motor, and backed out into the street. I watched the dust from his truck until I could no longer see it. Then I turned back to look at the street in front of my bench. It lay quiet and drowsing in the sun.

"It's going to be winter soon," I said. But I was talking to myself, for the street before me was empty.

Afterword

BY SARAH-MARIE HORNING

Hannah Jackson is a story about a woman, but it is also a history. Over the course of ninety vignettes narrated by thirteen different characters, a portrait of Hannah's life is pieced together from the varied perspectives and recollections of the people who knew her. The illustration of Hannah's life begins with a retelling of her funeral and slowly works backward to reveal the complexities of her life as she is perceived by others. The novel is primarily motivated by the tension surrounding the pivotal moment at which Hannah finds herself in social and spiritual crisis—when she falls in love with a married man. In a small, socially conservative Texas town, she finds herself spiritually at odds with the Reverend Stephen Longstreet, who, though conflicted about progressive cultural change, longs for a time when "the rules were more clearly defined." After Longstreet expels her from her church for adultery, Hannah struggles to regain the support of her faith and community. The depth of Hannah's spiritual and social isolation after this expulsion is intensified by the novel's fragmented structure that relays her story posthumously from the perspectives of the people in her family and community.

Begun in 1959 and completed in 1962, *Hannah Jackson* was constructed on the precipice of great cultural change in the United States, offering a reflection of a cultural tipping point at which social tensions erupted and second-wave feminism found its momentum. Eventually published in 1967, amid the politically turbulent 1960s, a novel about adultery in a small Texas town might seem out of step with a decade that was defined by rapid and sweeping social change. Texas has been infamously and variously described as a place where the cultures of the west and the old south meet. Set in the Texas Hill Country, *Hannah Jackson* unfolds amid a contentious mix of prejudicial and progressive attitudes. The characters in Sherry Kafka's novel are situated in a socially liminal space, and through their vignettes, the reader experiences the gradual and strained push-pull of these social attitudes on each of them, as they try to make meaning of Hannah's life and death within the context of their own nostalgia for the past and pessimism about the future—a cultural strain that defined end of the 1950s and boiled over into the political turmoil of the 1960s.

Many narratives of the cultural turn in the 1960s would suggest that only people on college campuses, people in major cities, or those already politically mobilized were active during that remarkable decade of social change, but *Hannah Jackson* helps illustrate that the changing attitudes that eventually developed in the decade were not isolated to liberal cities. The events of the late 1950s were socially and personally traumatic. The tensions of the Cold War, the investigations of the House Unamerican Activities Committee, Joe McCarthy's trials, the homophobia perpetuated by the "Lavender Scare," and the first US troops deployed to Vietnam in 1959 defined a time of heightened mistrust, bigotry, and alienation. These national traumas of the late 50s and early 60s serve as the backdrop for the characters as they reflect on their lives. These traumas and the generational traumas of the Great Depression and WWII are reflected in the individual stories that make up *Hannah Jackson*. In a later vignette, the character of Sye John Morrison who, disabled from a logging accident, watches the town from his bench, remarks "Fremond was changed by the Depression. Diminished, you might say. But it was shriveled by the war. There are more casualties come out of a war than are listed in the records and there are more places destroyed than ever see a battle." As the characters try to come to terms with these political and personal wounds, the fragmented vignettes speak in the language of trauma, in which memories are not linear, clearly defined narratives, but flashbulbs of visceral details or images of a traumatic event. Various characters struggle with suicide, PTSD, and other psychological responses to traumas so that in addition to the memories of Hannah as a spectral figure, memory and forgetting, ghosts and hauntedness figure prominently in the novel.

Processing the grief and psychological traumas of the first half of the twentieth century was a large part of social justice movements of the 1960s and is a significant force driving the novel, which is otherwise not plot driven. Kafka's decision to structure her work a novel of character—one that is driven by creating a detailed portrait of an individual rather than driven by events—places it in a long, progressive history of using portraiture as tool of social change. In his first "Lecture on Pictures" in 1861, Frederick Douglass wrote that photography would help make great strides toward developing the empathy and self-reflection required for abolitionist and civil rights progress: "Men of all conditions may see themselves as others see them." For Douglass, his faith in progress was linked to the possibility of photography as a tool for empathy building and critical vision. This same hope was shared by women photographers like Bettye Lane and Freda Leinwand, who used portraiture and photography to document the feminist and civil rights movements of the sixties. Novels, especially psychological novels that are constructed around character more than any other structural feature, can also do the work of portraits. *Hannah Jackson* is, no doubt, psychological portraiture. From the beginning, it draws the reader into reconstructing the life-story of its eponymous protagonist as other characters begin reflecting on her actions, choices, and motives. Told only from the point of view of others as they recall their various relationships with her after her funeral, Hannah is barred from speaking for herself as her community and family speculate about her life, making *Hannah Jackson*, as psychological novels are often described, the story of an "invisible life."

As the characters surmise and speculate about Hannah's motives, one wonders if her friends and family lack insight about Hannah because she has been made silent by multiple episodes of abandonment and betrayal. Early in her life, Hannah is abandoned by her mother who, in pursuit of an itinerate husband, leaves her in the care of a kind, older woman. From this point of abandonment, the people in her small Texas town seem to take on the work of caring for her as a community, each investing differently in her nurturance and development. By placing Hannah in the care of her community, and implicating them as responsible for her development, *Hannah Jackson* also operates as a feminist problem novel, opening up conversations not only about the ways women are often silenced in their communities, but also about kinship and other socialities, community care, intimate dependency and freedom, and about how American women in the mid-twentieth century negotiated the cultural change that was pushing them, ostensibly, toward greater freedom from social restraint.

At the heart of *Hannah Jackson* are serious stakes and questions about such relationships that contemporary feminist movements and scholarship,

like the works of Elizabeth Povinelli and Leah Lakshmi Piepzna-Sama-
rasinha, are grappling with today: How and when women exercise agency
or freedom in intimate dependency, and in what formulations does intimate dependency operate under social constraint? Contemporary feminist
scholarship is no longer simply asserting that the personal is political, but
asking when does intimate dependency cross the line from personal choice
to moral judgment (and in what forms do intimate social relationships
rightly or wrongly prompt moral sanctimoniousness)? How do the forces
of intimate dependencies, social structures, and the distribution of material conditions continue to interact? In negotiating this greater sexual freedom, Hannah, to the disdain of some in her community and to the delight
of others, is the aggressor in her successful pursuit of an older, married
man, Terrell. Like Professor Immanuel Rath (played by Curt Jurgens) in
the 1955 film *Blue Angel*, Terrell is drawn into an obsessive courtship with
Hannah that erodes his relationships, his social standing, and his dignity.
Terrell develops alcoholism, and the marriage with Hannah becomes
strained not only by the social consequences imposed on her as her church
and community make moral judgments about her relationship, but also
in the distribution of social and material capital for their children under
the strain of the great depression. Women, in this formulation of intimate
dependency, are in a double bind. Is she allowed to exhibit agency as a
seductress without being vilified or punished?

The feminist movement of the sixties was defined by a sexual and
social revolution for women in the United States and by a discourse of
love-affirming and life-affirming communitarianism. Far from faded into
history, the ideas and strategies out of second-wave feminism have gained
renewed attention in the first two decades of the twenty-first century,
as feminist pleasure activism and feminist somatics have built on these
initial formulations of bodily pleasure and "doing what feels good" as
sites of political resistance. Contemporary readers will surely identify in
Hannah Jackson the subversive agency that Hannah takes in pursuing a
married man. She resists the expectations of others even though she will
surely face social backlash. Contemporary readers may see Terrell as sim-
ilarly pleasure-seeking and performing a type of care work in his initial
emotional intimacy with Hannah. *Hannah Jackson* is a portrait of several
women characters—of Hannah as well as the women who serve as her
caregivers—who, with varying degrees of ambiguity, resist the gendered

expectations placed on them by their community. Like the reverend, who, in reflecting on Hannah's life and on his choice to remove her from the congregation, has undergone a countercultural transformation in his own spiritual thinking, the reader is tasked with engaging, assessing and reflecting on the events of Hannah's life. The result is an exercise in empathy and a litmus test of social values as the reader becomes complicit in the experience of assessing her choices against a set of cultural and spiritual values that either line up with or skew from those of the other characters.

A century after Frederick Douglass's hopeful remarks on the power of photography to orient narratives of American public culture toward empathy and social justice, Bettye Lane was assigned to cover the then emergent National Organization for Women and would go on to shoot iconic photographs of women's marches and portraits of now famous feminist leaders. On the last day of June in 1966, sixteen women, including Betty Friedan, gathered in a hotel room to draft the statement of purpose that would become the founding document for the National Organization for Women. Riding the momentum of the passage of the 1964 civil rights act, and steeped in the empathetic ethos of love-affirming and life-affirming discourses of the civil rights movement, the adopted statement called for "concrete action" as well as for the continued efforts of women to "create a new image of women," and to cultivate "their own equality, freedom, and human dignity." It is within this context that, with the depth and richness of a spiritual transformation, Sherry Kafka's *Hannah Jackson* reveals not only an empathetic image, but a complex narrative portrait of a woman caught between the rigid traditions of the early twentieth century and the rebellious attitudes that developed during the 1960s. In writing about "the problem that had no name" during the mid-1950s, Betty Friedan had been inspired by Simone de Beauvoir's historical and psychoanalytic study of the subjugation of women in *The Second Sex* (1949), to conduct a psychoanalytic study of her own to investigate why so many of her contemporaries were dissatisfied with their lives. Friedan's project, *The Feminine Mystique* (1963), is largely credited as a touchpoint for second-wave feminism partly because it marked a shift in feminist discourse away from mystification and toward thinking in terms of specific and embodied experiences. The collection of these experiences revealed that women's intimate relationships with men, and the abuses they experienced, were not idiosyncratic, but linked and systemic. This naming of the power of patriarchy was a fire starter that led to transformative feminist movements that explicitly took aim at exposing exploitative formulations of heteronormative intimate dependency.

Simultaneously validating Hannah's affair and portraying the devastating consequences of an inevitably unequal and fraught relationship, the novel is subversive in that it demonstrates complex formulations for women's agency. Hannah's character suggests that sexual exploitation and sexual agency for women can exist at the same time in the same relationship. Exploitative dynamics can and do shift or develop later in the relationship. Hannah's fraught marriage to Terrell suggests that female sexuality does not have to be binary—not just negotiated along the oppositions of victim/agent. Agency within intimate dependencies can be ambiguous and complex. In *Hannah Jackson*, the othering of Hannah's character has literally silenced her as a victim who is not allowed to speak for herself but has the assumptions of others projected onto her. At the same time, she is presented as resilient. As a character who negotiates and strategizes pathways for agency within her marriage. While the novel is structured around an affair, particularly one in which a young woman is rescued by a more experienced man, it does not rely on predictable tropes, but instead creates a complex relationship that brings up significant questions about the broader politics of physical and emotional intimacy.

Subversive in its handling of its eponymous character's marriage plot, *Hannah Jackson*, though, is not without its limitations. The novel is, ultimately, still a marriage plot, and marriage is presented as the only possible resolution to her coming-of-age. Hannah is presented as a strong character, but only in resistance to the authority of men. It is easy to read Terrell as paternalistic and self-serving, perhaps even predatory. Since he is married with children and Hannah is only in her late teens or early twenties when they initially begin their affair, it's quite possible to read the novel as romanticizing a paternalistic and predatory savior complex. It's also possible to read problematic dynamics of internalized sexism among the other women characters. Hannah's daughter, Secoria, judges her harshly at times, and Terrell's first wife conveniently lets Terrell end the marriage without any resistance.

None of this is to limit the feminist potential that *is* within *Hannah Jackson*: many of the characters, but especially the women, defy our expectations of them. Hannah's mother eschews the responsibilities of motherhood to follow an itinerate husband. Hannah's caretaker does the work of mothering despite fears and rumors that she is too old to be a mother. The women in *Hannah Jackson* are resistant and anarchical, they are generative and healers. These multiple possibilities and multiple interpretations, once contextualized in the sixties, reveal moments of growth and places where the possibilities for women still need to develop.

While the portrait of Hannah does the work of helping readers empathize with her motives and her social isolation, the subversive potential of *Hannah Jackson* also lies in its ability to position the reader simultaneously as empathetic and prejudiced. Read as foreshadowing the communitarian and love-affirming rhetoric that would develop and, in large part, come to define the sixties, Hannah's coming-of-age story becomes a journey of spiritual awakening and consciousness-raising not only for Hannah, but especially for the people in the town who are, in their rather vulnerable vignettes, posing to the reader their own self-reflections and reconfigurations during their period of mourning. Though their reflections reveal each character's progress toward a more empathetic view of Hannah's motives, the vignettes also reveal how each character gradually moves away from a position of prejudice. The reader, operating on only the retellings of others and not on actually hearing from Hannah herself, is forced into the prejudicial position of forming preconceived opinions. In fact, by positioning the reader as interpreter of Hannah's story using the perceptions of others, the novel is an experience in all types of prejudice.

Rapid cultural and social changes, however, don't always reflect personal transformations. *Hannah Jackson* remains relevant for its insightful portrait of a personal political transformation, and significant for its ability to implicate the reader into a position of prejudice. Anticipating current feminist applications of trauma studies to kyriarchy, *Hannah Jackson* offers not only feminist portraiture, but also a complex story of spiritual awakening that links multigenerational traumas to problems of patriarchy that extend beyond gender. Sherry Kafka's novel offers contemporary readers an opportunity to examine our own prejudices and willingness to rely on preconceived opinions. Most of all, *Hannah Jackson* offers lessons about love that model and encourage the work of spiritual awakening, spiritual growth, and nurturing spiritual growth in others.

About the Author

Sherry Kafka Wagner grew up in Arkansas. She studied with Paul Baker at Baylor University and attended the University of Iowa where this novel was developed. She was a Loeb Fellow at Harvard University, and she regularly consults nationally and internationally. She has published a play and children's books. *Photograph, author collection.*